"I Want A Chance To Talk To You Alone. No Business. Just Personal Stuff."

"No business? Justin, all we have between us is business." She didn't want to admit to herself or Justin that there was a spark of anything other than business fire between them.

"But we could have so much more. What harm could one drink do?"

"One drink," she repeated. Hell, who was she kidding, she was going to meet him. She wanted to get the measure of the man he was.

"Just one," he said. "I'll do my best to be charming and try to convince you to stay for more."

"I'm a tough cookie," she said.

"I think that's what you want the world to believe, but I bet there's a softer woman underneath all that."

But would she give him a chance to find out?

Dear Reader,

Family is essential to me, and I love writing books that involve a large family. My very first book for Desire, *The Bachelor Next Door,* was the first time I used alienation from a family as a conflict. In that book my hero's family was all dead and he was the last of his clan. In this book, Selena Gonzalez removed herself from her family because she felt guilty for falling in love with a con man and costing her family everything they owned.

Justin Stern and his brothers are close and have spent most of their lives together, but Justin is a bit of a loner. My sister Donna would say that's because he's the middle child. But I think it's also because of his personality. Justin likes to do things his own way. So falling in lust with his rival doesn't look like anything more than a minor setback to him.

Happy Reading!

Katherine

KATHERINE GARBERA

SEDUCING HIS OPPOSITION

Published by Silhouette Books

America's Publisher of Contemporary Romance

This book is dedicated to my son, Lucas, who continues to make me laugh with his insight and wit.

Acknowledgments:

Special thanks to my friend Francesca Galarraga, who answered some of my questions about the Cuban American community in South Florida. Any mistakes are my own.

SILHOUETTE BOOKS

ISBN-13: 978-0-373-73087-2

Recycling programs for this product may not exist in your area.

SEDUCING HIS OPPOSITION

Visit Silhouette Books at www.eHarlequin.com

Printed in U.S.A.

Books by Katherine Garbera

Silhouette Desire

†*His Wedding-Night Wager* #1708
†*Her High-Stakes Affair* #1714
†*Their Million-Dollar Night* #1720
The Once-A-Mistress Wife #1749
**Make-Believe Mistress* #1798
**Six-Month Mistress* #1802
**High-Society Mistress* #1808
The Greek Tycoon's Secret Heir #1845
The Wealthy Frenchman's Proposition #1851
The Spanish Aristocrat's Woman #1858
Baby Business #1888
§*The Moretti Heir* #1927
§*The Moretti Seduction* #1935
§*The Moretti Arrangement* #1943
Taming the Texas Tycoon #1952
‡*Master of Fortune* #1999
‡*Scandalizing the CEO* #2007
‡*His Royal Prize* #2014
††*Taming the VIP Playboy* #2068
††*Seducing His Opposition* #2074

†What Happens in Vegas…
**The Mistresses
*Sons of Privilege
§Moretti's Legacy
‡The Devonshire Heirs
††Miami Nights

KATHERINE GARBERA

is the *USA TODAY* bestselling author of more than forty books. She's always believed in happy endings and lives in Southern California with her husband, children and their pampered pet, Godiva. Visit Katherine on the web at www.katherinegarbera.com, or catch up with her on Facebook and Twitter.

Dear Reader,

Yes, it's true. We're changing our name! After more than twenty-five years of being part of Harlequin Enterprises, Silhouette Books will officially seal the merger by taking the company's name.

So if you notice a few changes on the covers starting April 2011—Silhouette Special Edition becoming Harlequin Special Edition, Silhouette Desire becoming Harlequin Desire, and Silhouette Romantic Suspense becoming Harlequin Romantic Suspense—don't be concerned.

We'll continue to have the same fantastic authors, wonderful stories, eye-catching covers and emotional, compelling reads. We're just going to be moving under the overall company name, which will make us even easier for you to see in the stores, on the internet and wherever you usually find us!

So look for the new logo, but remember, beneath the image will be the same promise of romantic stories of love, passion, adventure, family and a whole lot more. Just the way you like them!

Sincerely,

The Editors at Harlequin Books

One

Justin Stern pulled his Porsche 911 to a stop in the parking lot of the Miami-Dade County Zoning Offices. As the corporate attorney and co-owner of Luna Azul he was always busy and he liked that. Unlike his younger brother Nate, who was out partying every night and keeping the nightclub in the public eye, Justin preferred the quiet comfort of his office. He had worked hard to make sure that Luna Azul was where it was today from a financial perspective and he was determined to see it continue to grow.

That's what he was doing here today—ensuring that the future of the club didn't just rely on the nightclub crowd. He had negotiated the purchase of a strip mall that was run-down and in desperate need of repair. He'd researched the deed and found that it had changed hands about ten years ago and that had been the start of the disrepair of the buildings.

He envisioned an outdoor plaza with restaurants and shops that would help revitalize the area and bring a new revenue stream into the Luna Azul Company.

All he needed to do was file the final paperwork here today, and they could proceed with the expansion plans.

It was a beautiful spring morning, but he took no notice of it as he walked to the building. He took the stairs to the eleventh floor instead of the elevator because elevators really weren't an efficient use of time. He was happy to see there were only two other people in the waiting room. He took a number from the reception desk and then took a seat next to a very pretty Latina woman.

She had thick hair that curled around her face and shoulders in soft waves. Her skin was flawless, her olive complexion making her brown eyes seem even bigger. Her lips were full and pouty; he found he couldn't tear his eyes from her face until she raised one eyebrow at him.

"I'm not a creep," he said with a self-effacing grin. "You're just breathtaking."

She flushed and rolled her eyes. "As if I'd believe that line."

"Why wouldn't you?" he asked, turning to face her.

"I'm used to smooth-talking men," she said. "I can spot one a mile away."

"Just because I'm complimenting you doesn't mean that I'm BSing you," he said. She was really lovely and he liked the soft sound of her voice. She was well put together. He had no idea of designers or fashion but her clothes looked nice—feminine. For the first time in a very long time he didn't mind having to wait.

"I suspect you can be very charming when you put your mind to it," she said.

"Perhaps," he said. "Not really. I'm usually straight to the point."

"You don't strike me as blunt," she said.

"I am," he said. He wasn't giving her a line—she really was gorgeous. She had caught his eye and distracted him. And he didn't mind at all. That was the surprising part for him. "Your eyes…are so big, I could get lost in them."

"Your eyes are so blue that they look like the waters in Fiji."

He laughed out loud. "Is that what I sound like to you?"

"Yes," she said with a smile. "Honestly, I'm not all that."

She was all that and a lot more, but he wasn't the best when it came to talking to women. In a corporate boardroom or at a negotiating table he was the best but one-on-one when he was interested in a girl…well that was when he got caught up.

"What brings you here?" he asked, then shook his head. "Zoning."

"Zoning," she said at the same time. "I'm here to file an injunction.

"Is it for your own company or a client?" he asked, wanting to know more.

"My grandparents think that an outside company is trying to buy their property and turn it into some big commercial club. So I'm checking it out for them."

"Do you live here in Miami then? Or just your grandparents?"

"My entire family lives here," she said. "But I live in New York."

"Oh. So ours will have to be a long-distance relationship," he said.

She raised her eyebrow at him. "This relationship might not make it out of the waiting room."

"I'm not giving up on us so easily," he said.

"Good. One of us should fight for this," she said, deadpan.

"I guess it will be me," he said with a grin. He couldn't help it. Something about this woman just made him smile.

A nattily dressed man came to the counter. "Number fifteen."

She glanced at the paper in her hand. "That's me."

"Just my luck. Any chance you'll give me your number?"

She tucked a thick strand of her hair behind her ear and reached into her handbag. "Here's my card. My cell number is on the bottom."

"I will call you," he said.

"I hope so…what's your name?"

"Justin," he said standing up and taking the card from her, but he didn't look at it. "Justin Stern. And what should I call you other than beautiful?"

She was quiet a moment as she looked him over, a light going on in her eyes. "Selena," she said. "Selena Gonzalez."

She walked away and he watched every sway of her hips. Then her name registered. Gonzalez was the last name of Tomas's big-gun lawyer and granddaughter. Selena Gonzalez…wait a minute; he was lusting after the corporate lawyer Tomas Gonzalez had called in from New York to stop his plans for the strip mall.

That wasn't cool.

Dammit, he wanted to call her. It wasn't very often

he met a woman who got his rather odd sense of humor and could banter with him. But now…

Then again, she didn't live here. She was in town for a few weeks at most, he thought. That made her the perfect woman for him.

Was he out of his mind? She was gumming up the plans he'd worked hard for. And if she was anything like her grandfather, she'd be stubborn and unwilling to realize that change was necessary if they were going to keep their section of Calle Ocho alive and kicking.

Selena Gonzalez left the zoning board with the information she needed and an injunction in hand. The emergency call from her grandfather three days ago made it sound like there was going to be a big bad company trying to take away her grandparents' market. From the information she just received…well, she still wasn't sure.

Justin Stern had intrigued her and made her wish that he was a stranger. But she'd heard enough about the smooth-talking rich boy who was trying to muscle out her grandparents to know that Justin wasn't the Mr. Congenial he had portrayed in the waiting room.

If the Luna Azul Company did succeed in developing the old strip mall that housed her grandparents' business now she had a feeling their neighborhood would change. She'd seen the plans that had been submitted by the company—they showed an upscale shopping area designed to bring tourists into the neighborhood. That wasn't what her grandparents' Latin American grocery store was about, but it wasn't the nightclub they feared would be built, either.

As she drove home, she took in the lush, tropical sights of Miami. Her family had wanted her home for a long time. She acknowledged to herself that if it hadn't been for this legal emergency she'd still be ignoring their pleas.

This area made her…it made her all the things that she didn't like about herself. When she was home she was impulsive and passionate. And made stupid decisions—like giving her number to a handsome stranger in a waiting room.

And after all that had happened with Raul ten years ago, she'd been afraid to come back home. She hadn't wanted to face her past or the memories that lingered everywhere she went in her old home and her old neighborhood. As she parked in front of her grandparents' house, she drew a deep breath.

"Did you get the injunction?" her grandfather asked, the minute she stepped through the door.

He wasn't an overly tall man—probably no more than five-eleven. Life had been good to Tomas Gonzalez and he wore his success with a gently rounded stomach. He could be tough as nails in business but he always had a smile for his family and a hug and kiss for her. One of fifteen grandchildren that lived in a three-block radius of his house, Selena had always felt well loved in this home. Especially after her parents' death eleven years ago. A drunk driver had taken both of her parents from her in one accident, leaving her little brother and her alone to face the world. Her grandparents had stepped in but it hadn't been the same.

"I did, *abuelito*," she said. "And tomorrow I will go down to the Luna Azul Company offices and talk to them about our terms if they still want to go ahead with their plans."

She sat down at the large butcher-block table in the kitchen. The kitchen was the one room where they spent most of their time at her grandparents' house. Her grandmother was in the other room watching her shows.

"Very good, *tata*. I told you we needed you," he said. *Tata* was his nickname for her—just a sweet little endearment that made her feel loved every time he used it. "Those Stern brothers think they can come in and buy up all our property but they aren't part of our community."

"*Abuelito,* the Luna Azul Company has been a part of the community for ten years. From what they told me in the zoning office, they've done a lot for our community."

Her grandfather threw his hands up in the air. "Nothing, *tata,* that's what they have done for our community."

She laughed at him. She was used to his being passionate, even melodramatic about Little Havana. Her grandfather was part of the pre-communist Cuba—an energetic and creative environment—and he'd brought that with him to Miami when he'd become an exile. He still talked about Cuba with fond memories. It was a Cuba that no longer existed, but his stories were always enjoyable.

"What are you two laughing at?" her grandmother asked, coming in to refill her espresso cup with sugar and coffee.

"Those Stern brothers," her grandfather said. "I think Selena is just what we need to keep them in their place."

Her grandmother sat down beside her. She smelled of coffee and the gardenia perfume she'd always worn. She wrapped her arm around Selena's shoulder. "You promised to stay until summer, *tata*. Will you be able to take care of all this by then?"

She hugged her grandmother back. "Definitely. I want to make sure that you get the most out of this new development."

"Good. We want to own our market…the way we used to," Grandfather said.

Selena felt a pang around her heart as she realized that the reason they didn't own their own market was because of her. They were mere renters in the market the Sterns planned to develop, but once they had owned the place. Until Selena messed everything up. She had to make this right for them. "I met Justin Stern at the zoning office. So I will set up a meeting with him," Selena assured her grandparents.

"Good," her grandmother said. "I am going back to my shows. Are you staying at your house?"

"I haven't decided yet," she said. She still owned a house here. She didn't know if she wanted to go back and stay in it all alone. But staying here wasn't a solution; after living alone for so long, she needed her space.

She shrugged. "What's the use of owning a house if you never use it."

"I will send Maria over to make sure it's clean and ready for you," her grandmother said.

"That's not necessary," Selena said. Her grandparents were the caretakers of the old Florida house while she was in New York. It was the house she'd lived in with Raul while they'd both been in school at the University of Miami. There were a lot of memories in that place.

"I can clean it out if I need to," Selena said.

"No. We will make it ready for you. You concentrate on Luna Azul and Justin Stern," Grandfather said.

She shook her head. "He's a very charming man, *abuelita*. Have you met him?"

"No, but *abuelito* has, several times. You find him shrewd, right?" her grandmother said, turning to her husband.

"*Si*. Very shrewd and very…he watches people and then he makes an offer that is exactly right for you. He's like the devil."

Selena laughed, thinking that her grandfather's observation was spot on. "He is silver-tongued."

"*Si*. Watch yourself, *tata*. You don't want to fall for another man like that," her grandfather said.

She wrapped an arm around her own waist as her grandmother got to her feet and yelled at her grandfather in Spanish, telling him to let sleeping dogs lie. Selena quietly left the kitchen, going into the backyard and finding a seat on the bench nestled between blooming hibiscus plants underneath a large tree covered with orchids.

She'd stayed away for so long because of Raul and everything that had happened between them. But now that she was back she was going to have to face her past and really move on from it. Not run away as she'd done before. And she liked the thought of focusing on Justin Stern. He was just the man she needed to forget the past and start to live again here.

Justin signed a few papers that were waiting for his signature and then sent his administrative assistant out for lunch. *An injunction*. Selena Gonzalez with her sexy body and big eyes had filed an injunction against the company to keep them from beginning with their construction work until they proved that they were using local vendors. Now their plans for a ground-breaking in conjunction with the tenth anniversary gala was going to be slowed down if not halted.

"Got a minute?"

Justin glanced up to see his older brother Cameron standing in the doorway. Cam was dressed in business casual, as was his way. He was the one who ran the club and made sure the business there was on track. Unlike Justin, who always wore a suit and spent the majority of his time at his office here in the downtown high-rise complex.

"Sure. What's up?"

"How'd things go at the zoning office?" Cam asked, coming inside and sitting down in one of the leather armchairs in front of his desk.

"Not so good. The Gonzalez family filed an injunction against the building. I'm going to spend the afternoon working on the paperwork we need to file in response. I'm hoping to speak with their lawyer later and see if we can negotiate some kind of deal."

"Damn. I wanted to have the ground-breaking at the tenth anniversary celebration. I was also hoping we could maybe sign up some new, high-profile tenants, but this could put a damper on things."

"I will do what I can to make it happen. Don't get your hopes up, the neighbors and existing tenants in that market don't like us."

"Use your charm to convince them otherwise," Cam said.

"I'm not charming."

"Hell, I know that. You should send Myra."

"My assistant?"

"Yes, she's friendly and everyone likes her."

She was nice, but she didn't have the right kind of

experience to talk to the current occupants of the strip mall and make them understand what was needed.

"I'll head over there after I talk to Selena."

"Who is Selena?"

"Tomas Gonzalez's lawyer."

"Sounds like all the opening you need to get them on our team."

"Stop trying to manipulate me into doing what you want," he warned his brother.

"Why? I'm good at it."

Justin threw a mock punch at Cam who pretended to take the hit.

"Go. I have real work to do," Justin said.

"I will."

Cam left and Justin leaned back in his chair. He had plenty of business to keep him occupied but instead he was thinking of Selena Gonzalez—the lawyer and the woman.

His intercom buzzed. "There's a Ms. Gonzalez on line one."

Speak of the devil. He clicked over to the correct line. "This is Justin," he said.

"Hello, there."

"Hi. I must be remembering our conversation wrong," he said.

"I know I said I'd let you call but I've never been one of those women who waits for a man." Her voice was just as lovely over the phone as it had been in person. He closed his eyes and let the sound of it wash over him. She was distracting. And he needed to keep her from shaking him from his target.

"I'm glad to hear that. I thought you might be difficult given that you filed an injunction against me."

"That wasn't personal, Justin," she said. And he liked the way his name sounded on her lips.

"Yes, it was, Selena. What can I do for you?"

"I didn't realize we had mutual interests," she said. "When we met, I mean."

"I know what you meant…by mutual interests do you mean we both want to ensure that the Latin market is a vibrant part of the community?

"I want to make sure that some big-deal club owner doesn't take the community heritage and bastardize it for his own good."

"I guess you're not coming in here with any pre-conceived notions," he said wryly.

"No, I'm not, I know exactly what kind of man I'm up against. My *abuelito* said you are a silver-tongued devil and I should watch myself around you."

"Selena, you have nothing to fear from me," he said. "I'm a very fair businessman. In fact, I think your *abuelito* will be very happy with my latest offer."

"Send it to me and I will let you know."

"Come down to my office so we can talk in person. I prefer that to emails and faxes."

He leaned back in his chair. He knew how to negotiate, and having Selena here on his own turf was the way for him to get what he wanted. No one could turn him down once he started talking. To be honest, he'd never had a deal go south once he got the other party in the same room with him.

"Okay, when?"

"Today if you have time."

"Can you hold on?"

"Sure," he said. The line went silent and he turned to look out his plate-glass windows. The skyline of downtown Miami was gorgeous and he appreciated how lucky he was to live in paradise.

"Okay, we can do it today."

"We?"

"My *abuelito* and I."

"Great. I look forward to seeing Tomas again."

"And what about me?" she asked.

"I've thought of little else but seeing you again."

She laughed. "I'm tempted to believe you, but I know you are a businessman and business must always come first."

She was right. He wanted her to be different but the truth of the matter was that he was almost thirty-five and set in his ways. There was little doubt that someday he might want to settle down but it wasn't today.

And it wouldn't be with Selena.

"Good girl," he said.

"Girl?"

"I didn't mean that in a condescending way."

"How did you mean it?" she asked.

He had no idea if he'd offended her or not. "Just teasingly. Maybe I should stick to business. I'm much better at knowing what not to say."

She laughed again and he realized how much he liked the sound of that. He thought it prudent to get off the phone with her before he said something else that could put the entire outdoor plaza project at risk.

"I'll see you then. How does two o'clock sound?" he said.

"We'll be there," she agreed and hung up.

Two

As Selena and her grandfather left for their meeting, her other relatives were arriving to start cooking the dinner. Since she hadn't been home in almost ten years, the entire Gonzalez clan was getting together for a big feast.

To some people coming home might mean revisiting the place they had grown up, for her coming home meant a barbeque in the backyard of her grandparents' house and enough relatives to maybe require an occupancy permit.

Being a Gonzalez was overwhelming. She had forgotten how much she enjoyed the quiet of her life in Manhattan until this moment. This was part of what she'd run from. In Miami everyone knew her, in Manhattan she was just another person on the street.

She had the top down on her rental Audi convertible and the Florida sunshine warmed her head and the breeze stirred her hair as they drove to Justin Stern's office.

Having the top down did something else. It made conversation with her *abuelito* nearly impossible and right now she needed some quiet time to think. Though Justin Stern had flirted with her, she knew he was one sharp attorney and she'd need to have her wits about her when they talked.

"Selena?"

"Si?"

"You missed the turnoff," her grandfather said.

"I…dang it, I wasn't paying attention."

"What's on your mind?"

"This meeting. I want to make sure you and *abuelita* are treated fairly."

"You will, *tata.*"

She made a U-turn at the next intersection and soon they were in the parking lot of Luna Azul Company's corporate headquarters. The building was large and modern but fit the neighborhood, and as she walked closer, Selena noticed that it wasn't new construction but had been a remodel. She made a mental note to check on this building and to investigate if having the Stern brothers here had enhanced this area.

"You ready, *abuelito?*"

"For what?"

"To take on Justin."

"Hell, yes. I've been doing it the best I can, but…we needed you," her grandfather said.

They entered the air-conditioned building. The receptionist greeted them and directed them to the fifth floor executive offices.

"Hello, Mr. Gonzalez."

"Hello, Myra. How are you today?" her grandfather

asked the pretty young woman who greeted them there.

"Not bad. Hear you've brought a big-gun lawyer to town," she said.

"I brought our attorney. Figured it was about time I had someone who could argue on Mr. Stern's level."

Myra laughed and even Selena smiled. She could tell that her grandfather had been doing okay negotiating for himself. Why had he called her?

"I'm Selena Gonzalez," Selena said stepping forward and holding out her hand.

"Myra Temple," the other woman said. "It's nice to meet you. You will be meeting in the conference room at the end of the hall. Can I get either of you something to drink?"

"I'll have a sparkling water," her grandfather said.

"Me, too," Selena said and followed her grandfather down the hall to the conference room.

The walls were richly paneled and there was a portrait of Justin and two other men who had to be his brothers. There was a strong resemblance in the stubborn jawline of all the men. She recognized Nate Stern, Justin's younger brother and a former New York Yankees baseball player.

Her *abuelito* sat down but she walked around the room, and checked out the view from the fifth floor and then the model for the Calle Ocho market center.

"Have you seen this, *abuelito*?"

He shook his head and came over to stand next to her. The Cuban American market that her grandparents owned was now replaced with a chain grocery store. She was outraged and angry.

"I can't believe this," Selena said.

"You can't believe what?" Justin asked as he entered

the conference room. Myra was right behind him with a tray of Perrier and glasses filled with ice cubes.

"That you think replacing the Cuban American market with a chain grocery store would be acceptable."

"To be honest we haven't got an agreement with them yet," Justin said. "This is just an artist's concept of how the Market will look."

"Well the injunction I filed today is going to hamper your agreement with them."

"It will indeed. That's why I invited you here to talk."

She was disgusted that she had fallen for his sexy smile and self-deprecating charm at the zoning office because she saw now that he was a smooth operator. And she'd had her fill of them when she was younger. It made her angry to think that in ten years she hadn't learned not to fall for that kind of guy.

"Then let's get to work," she said. "I've drawn up a list of concerns."

"I look forward to seeing them," Justin said. "And Tomas, it's nice to see you again," he said, shaking the older man's hand.

"I'd prefer it if we could stop meeting," Tomas said.

"To be fair I'd like that, too. I want to move this project forward," Justin said.

She bet he did, he was probably losing money with each day that they waited to break ground on their new market. But she was here to make sure that he realized that he couldn't come in and replace traditional markets with a shiny upscale shopping area with no ties to the community.

"What is your largest concern?" he asked. "This was a Publix supermarket strip mall before you first came to it, Tomas. So you have had chain grocers in the neighborhood before. We can invite another retailer if you'd prefer that."

Selena realized that Justin didn't necessarily understand what their objection to his building in the community truly was.

"Justin, this strip mall is part of the Cuban American community. Our family's store isn't just a place for people to pick up groceries, it's where the old men come in the morning for their coffee and then sit around and discuss the business of the day. It's a place where young mothers bring their kids to play in the back and have great Cuban food.

"This is the heart of the neighborhood. You can't just rip it out."

Justin knew this meeting wasn't going to be easy. He'd figured that out the moment he met Selena. She was the kind of woman that made a man work for it. And he knew that she was looking out for the interests of her community and to be fair he needed that community to want to shop there. Even though they'd do a good crossover business from the club and he had an arrangement with some local tour companies to add the new Luna Azul Market to their tourist stops once it opened, it would be the neighborhood residents that would make or break this endeavor.

"I'm open to your suggestions. So far Tomas has only demanded that we leave the strip mall the way it is and I think that we both know that isn't a solution."

"We both don't know that," she said.

"Have you been down to the property lately?" he asked her. "The mall is old and run-down. The families that you speak of are dwindling, isn't that right, Tomas?"

Tomas shrugged but then glanced over at Selena.

"The buildings need repairs and the landlord…you, Justin, should be making them."

"I want to make more than repairs. I'm not even sure if they meet the new hurricane wind resistance standards."

Selena pulled out a notebook and started writing on it. "We will check into it. Have you considered forming a committee with the community leaders and your company?"

"We've had a few informal discussions."

"You need to do a lot more than that. Because if you want the neighborhood support you are going to have to open a dialogue with them."

"Okay," Justin said. "But only if you serve on the committee."

She blinked up and then tipped her head to the side. "I don't think that I need to be on there."

"I do," Justin said. "You grew up there, and are also familiar with the legal and zoning issues. You will be able to see the bigger picture."

"I don't think—"

"I agree with him, *tata,* you should be on there," Tomas said.

"Tata?" Justin asked, smiling.

She glared at her grandfather. "It's a nickname."

She blushed, and it was the first crack he'd seen in her all-business, tough-as-nails shell.

The business deal was going to go through whether Tomas and his allies wanted it to or not. Justin had already scheduled a round of golf with the zoning commissioner, Maxwell Strong, at the exclusive club he belonged to to get him to change his mind. And over the next week he'd work on finding a way out of the legal hole that Selena had dug for him. But he wanted to see more of her.

And this committee thing would be perfect. Plus, he did actually want the community behind the project. "Myra, will you set up a meeting time for us...I think we should use Luna Azul. Tomas and Selena will send you a list of people to invite."

"I'd like to take a closer look at the plans for the market," Selena said.

"I'll leave you two to discuss that," Tomas said. "I need to call around and see when everyone will be available to meet."

"Myra will show you to an office you can use," Justin said.

After Tomas and Myra left the room, Justin studied Selena for a minute. Her head was bent and she was making notes on her legal pad. He noticed that her handwriting was very neat and very feminine.

"Why are you staring at me?"

"I thought I already told you that I like the way you look."

"That wasn't just you trying to...I don't know what you were up to. Did you know who I was in that lobby of the zoning office?"

He shook his head. "No. I wish I had known."

"Why?"

"Maybe I could have talked you out of filing that injunction," he said with a laugh.

She chuckled at that. "Wow, that's putting a lot of pressure on your supposed charm."

He grabbed his side pretending she'd wounded him. "Good thing I'm tough-skinned."

"You'd have to be in order to work in the neighborhood you do. How did you and your brothers manage to make

Luna Azul a success without getting the community behind you?" she asked him.

"Some locals do frequent the club but we rely on the celebs for business. They bring in their own crowd of followers. We book first-rate bands and we have salsa lessons in the rooftop club...so we do okay. Have you ever been there?"

She shook her head. "I left Miami before you opened your doors."

"Why did you leave?" he asked.

"None of your business," she replied with a tight look that told him he'd somehow gone too far.

"My apologies. I expected you to say you needed some freedom...would you have dinner with me tonight?"

"Why?"

"I believe in keeping my enemies close."

"Me, too," she said.

"I'll take that as a yes."

"It is a yes. But I'll pick the place." She wrote an address at the bottom of her legal pad and then tore the paper off and handed it to him. "Be there at seven. Dress casual."

"Do I need to bring anything?"

"Just your appetite."

She gathered her things and then stood up and walked out of the conference room. He watched her leave.

Inviting Justin to her family get-together was inspired. He wanted to do business in this community but he didn't understand it. This would be his lesson.

On her way home, she'd driven down to the strip mall to see her grandfather's store, and it had been run-down more than she expected.

Something was needed, but an outlet mall or a high-end shopping plaza wasn't it. The Calle Ocho neighborhood leaders wouldn't stand for. Plus, she wanted to ensure that her grandparents got the best deal possible.

They had always been at the center of things in Little Havana and she wasn't about to let Justin Stern take that away from them.

She also stopped by her house. When she entered, she was swamped with memories but managed to brush them aside as she freshened up and got ready to walk back over to her grandparents'. The last thing she wanted was to be here, she realized. She packed a bag with some clothes she found in the closet, locked the house and pointed her rented convertible toward the beach.

Her New York law practice had made her a wealthy woman. And considering this was the first real break she'd taken from work in the last eight years she thought she deserved a treat. All she did was work and save her money. Well that wasn't completely true—she did have an addiction to La Perla lingerie that wouldn't stop. But for the most part all she did was work.

So as she pulled up at the Ritz and asked for a suite for the next month, Selena knew she was doing the right thing. She was in luck and was soon ensconced in memory-free luxury. Just what she needed.

As she was settling in, her cell phone rang and she glanced at the number. It was a local number but not one she recognized. She answered it anyway. "This is Selena."

"This is Justin. How about if we have drinks at Luna Azul first so you can see the club?"

"No."

"Just a flat-out no, you aren't going to even pretend to think it over," he said.

"That's right. I am not staying near there, anyway. I'm at the Ritz," she said. She was kicked back on the love seat in her living room reading up on Justin on her laptop.

"How about a drink in the lobby bar?" he suggested. His voice was deep over the phone—very sexy.

"Why?" she asked. She wasn't sure spending any time alone with him was the right thing. She wanted to keep it all business between them. That was the only way she was going to keep herself from acting on the attraction she felt for him.

"I want a chance to talk to you alone. No business— just personal stuff."

"No business? Justin, all we have between us is business." She hoped that making that statement out loud would somehow make it true. She didn't want to admit to herself or Justin that there was a spark.

"But we could have so much more."

"Ha! You don't even know me," she said.

"That's exactly what I'm hoping to change. What harm could one drink do?"

"One drink," she repeated. Hell, who was she kidding? She was going to meet him. She'd invited him to her welcome-home party so he could get to know her family and not only because of business. She wanted to see how he was with them to get the measure of the man he was.

"Just one," he said. "I'll do my best to be charming and try to convince you to stay for more."

"I'm a tough cookie," she said.

"I think that's what you want the world to believe but I bet there's a softer woman underneath all that."

She hoped he never found out. She had tried so hard to bury the woman—*girl*—she'd been when she'd graduated from the University of Miami and left her hometown behind. Were there still any vestiges of that passionate side of her left after Raul had broken her heart?

Sure she dated, but she was careful that it was just casual, never letting her emotions get involved. Raul had taught her that the price to be paid for loving foolishly wasn't one that only she paid. Her grandparents had almost lost their business because of her poor judgment in men, and Selena had vowed to never be that weak again.

"Pretty much what you see is what you get with me," she said, uncomfortable talking about herself. "What about you? Are you all awkward charm and sleek business acumen?"

He laughed. "I guess so. It's hard when you grow up with a charismatic brother—everyone just expects you to be the same."

"How many brothers do you have?" she asked. Though she'd spent the afternoon reading about them on the internet she wanted to hear how he described his family. She had no idea what it had been like to grow up the son of a wealthy, semi-famous pro golfer or to have a brother who played for the Yankees. "I know your dad played pro golf."

"Yes, he did. I have two brothers…"

"That's right. And you're the middle one?"

"Yes, ma'am. The quiet one."

"I haven't seen you quiet yet."

He laughed again and she liked the sound of it—a little too much. No matter how charming he was she wasn't going to let him past her guard. She had to take control and remind him that they were doing things on her terms. "Okay, so one drink. Why don't you come by around—"

"Five. We can have hors d'oeuvres, too."

"Five? That's two hours before our date. How are you going to make one drink last that long?" she asked, but she was already getting up and starting to ready herself to meet him. It was only forty minutes until five.

"If things go well I don't want to cheat you out of spending time alone with me."

"You are so thoughtful," she said.

"I am. It's one of my many gifts."

"I'll remember that when we are doing our negotiations for the marketplace," she said with a laugh. "Five o'clock in the Ritz lobby bar."

"See you there," he said and hung up.

She went into the bedroom and looked at herself in the mirror. She looked like she'd just come from work. She opened her closet and realized she had a closet full of casual and work clothes. Not exactly the sexiest clothing in the world.

Did she want to look sexy for her date with Justin?

"Yes," she said, looking at herself in the mirror. If she was going to get the upper hand on Justin she was going to need to pull out all the stops.

It sure was going to be fun to go head-to-head with Mr. Know-Your-Enemies.

Three

Justin valet-parked his car and walked into the lobby of the Ritz on South Beach. The view from the restaurant here was breathtaking and easily one of the best in this area. He glanced at his watch. He was a few minutes early and as he scanned the lobby he didn't see Selena.

He walked to the lobby bar and found seating for two in a relatively quiet area. He knew that he had to get to know Selena better for business reasons. He had to know how she thought so he could make sure he made the right offer—one she'd accept so that he could get the market back on track. He hadn't gotten the Luna Azul Company to where it was today by not knowing how to read people.

But he wasn't going to deny that he wanted Selena. There had been a moment in the conference room this afternoon when he'd wished they were alone so he could pull her into his arms and see if he could crack her reserve with passion.

"Justin?"

He glanced over his shoulder and felt like he'd been sucker punched. The prim, reserved woman he'd flirted with was gone and in her place was a bombshell. Maybe it was just her thick ebony hair hanging in waves around her shoulders, or the red lipstick that drew his eyes to her full mouth. But his gut insisted that it was the curve-hugging black dress she wore that ended midthigh. He skimmed his gaze down to her dainty-looking ankles and those high-heeled strappy sandals that made him almost groan out loud.

"Selena," he said, but his voice sounded husky and almost choked to him.

She arched one eyebrow and smiled. "Happy to see me?"

"That is an understatement. Let me get us a drink. What's your poison?"

"Mojito, I think. I need something to cool me down."

He signaled the cocktail waitress and placed their drink order before diving right in. "Tell me about yourself, Selena. Why are you living in New York when your family is still here?"

"No small talk?" she asked, turning her attention away from him and skimming the room.

"Why bother with that?" he asked. "We both want to know as much about each other as we can, right?"

"Definitely. I just didn't plan on going first," she said with a smile as she turned back to face him again.

Every time she talked he tried to concentrate on her words but he couldn't take his eyes from her lips. He wanted to know how they would feel under his own.

What kind of kisser would she be? Would she taste as good as he imagined?

"I'm a gentleman," he said. And he didn't want to show her any weakness.

"So it's ladies first?" she asked.

"In all things, especially pleasure," he said.

She blushed as their waitress arrived with the drinks. She started to take a sip but he stopped her.

"A toast to new relationships."

"And a quick resolution to our business problems," she said.

He clinked his glass to hers and watched as she took a swallow of her cocktail. When she took the glass from her mouth she licked her lips and he felt his blood begin to flow a little heavier in his veins as his groin stirred.

He wanted her.

That wasn't news. But sitting here with her in the bar was starting to seem like a really dumb idea. He needed all his wits about him because it was apparent that Selena was playing with her A-game and he needed to as well.

"You were going to tell me all your secrets," he said.

She laughed. "I was going to tell you the official version of my life."

"I'll take whatever you offer," he said.

"I bet you will. Okay, where to start?"

"The beginning," he suggested, shifting his legs to make room in his pants for his growing erection.

"Birth?"

"Nah, skip to college. I did a little internet research on you and saw that you graduated from the University of Miami. What made you choose to go to Fordham Law

School instead of choosing something closer to home?" he asked.

"I needed a change of scene. I was pretty sure that I wanted to practice corporate law and I had done an internship for one summer with the firm that I work for now. So it made sense to go there."

"That's about the same time your grandparents sold the marketplace and switched over to being renters in the space. Did they do that to pay for your education?" he asked.

Her face got very tight and she shook her head. "I had a scholarship."

"I did a deed search to see who had owned the property before the previous owner and it was your grandfather. I can't understand why he sold," Justin continued. He really wanted to know why ten years ago, Tomas had made the decision to sell the marketplace property and become a rental tenant instead. That made no sense to Justin as a businessman. But it also made no sense based on what he knew of Tomas. Tomas liked being his own boss.

"What about you? Harvard law graduates can usually write their own ticket to any law firm but you came back home and worked with your brothers instead, why?"

Justin stretched back and looked at her for a minute. That was complicated. He couldn't tell her that coming back was the hardest decision he'd ever made because even his brothers didn't know that.

"They needed me," he said. It was close to the truth. He didn't hold with outright lies.

He took another sip of his drink and then leaned forward. "Why are you here now?"

"My grandfather said you were too slick and he couldn't trust you."

"That's hardly true. Tomas is very shrewd. And don't change the subject. Why did he sell the marketplace if not for your education?"

She flushed and her hand trembled for a minute and then she took a sip of her drink.

He waited for her to answer but she didn't say anything.

"Selena?"

"That is a private matter and I won't discuss it with you."

Selena was surprised that he'd dug back on the deed. But she shouldn't have been. She may have momentarily distracted Justin with her clothing and changed appearance but he'd adjusted quickly by pulling the rug out from under her with that question.

"Okay. I can respect that. I was just thinking that if they hadn't sold the property perhaps it wouldn't be so derelict now," Justin said.

He was right. Selling that property had been a mistake and that was why she was here. To right the wrong she'd caused when she'd allowed herself to get suckered by a smooth-talking con man ten years ago.

She'd never seen him coming, Raul had swept her off her feet, and then once she'd fallen for his sweet talk, he'd used that love she had for him against her. The con he'd run on her had been simple enough. He was starting his own company, a luxury yacht business, and needed some initial investors. She'd put all of the inheritance she'd gotten from her parents into it, and in a calculated move on Raul's part she'd convinced her grandparents to mortgage the market and invest, as well. Raul took all the money and disappeared overnight.

The ensuing investigation into Raul's disappearance

had been an upheaval in their lives. It had taken almost two years to get it sorted out and at the end with lawyers' fees and private investigator charges her grandparents had no money left. They were forced to sell the marketplace and become renters. Raul was eventually caught and brought to justice, but their money was never repaid.

It had been one of the most humiliating times of her life and she'd been very glad to escape Miami to Fordham where she knew no one. She'd started over and been very careful since then not to let her emotions get the better of her.

"You are very right," she said. She took another sip of her mojito. The smooth rum and mint drink was soothing. Justin watched her each time she swallowed and she knew she'd been distracting him all evening.

She liked the feeling of power it gave her to know that she could manipulate him. She wondered if that was what Raul had felt as he'd slowly drawn her into his web. Had it been the power? She hadn't thought of that in years, but her experiences with men had taught her that in all relationships—personal and business—it all came down to who had something the other wanted. And right now, she had something that Justin wanted a lot.

"I know," he said. He was cocky and she had to admit that it was a trait she was beginning to enjoy in him.

He seemed so in control. She'd been told she gave that impression, as well, but she knew underneath her professional persona she was usually a mess. Was it the same for him? But she couldn't detect any chinks in his armor. She was starting to realize that even distracted he was going to be a tough opponent.

She leaned forward to place her drink on the table

and noticed his eyes tracked down toward her breasts. She shifted her shoulders so the fabric of her dress drew the material taut over her curves and then sat back.

"Have you thought of selling the property back to my grandparents? I think that would be the easiest solution." Then she could conclude this business in Miami and take the first flight back to New York and her nice, safe, regular life. A place where the businessmen she encountered looked dull and gray like a Manhattan winter instead of like Justin, who was tan, vibrant and hot…just like Miami.

"I don't think so," he said, looking back up at her eyes. "Your grandparents don't…"

"What?"

"They don't have the resources to make the property profitable the way that the Luna Azul Company does. I mean, they would probably fix up their market but it is going to take a lot of capital to revamp the entire area. And that is the only way you are going to keep your current clientele and get new customers."

He had a point but she didn't like the thought of an outsider owning the market. It also irked her that this situation was entirely her fault. If she hadn't fallen for Raul so many years ago, her beloved *abuelito* wouldn't have to deal with the Stern brothers on their terms.

"Granted but if you take away the local feel of the marketplace, you will lose money."

"That's where you come in. I liked your idea of forming a committee. I wish I'd thought of it sooner," Justin said. "But enough business. I want to know the woman behind the suit. I like your dress by the way."

She tossed her hair and made herself let go of the work part of being with Justin. There was nothing to be accomplished tonight. He'd either come around to her way of thinking or he'd find out how many complications she could put in the way of his business deals.

"I noticed you liking it."

"Good. Are you finished with your drink?"

"Why?"

"I want to take you for a walk along the beach."

"I'd like that," she said, getting to her feet. "I miss the beach."

"I live right on it. That was one thing that motivated me to come back home after Harvard. I like living somewhere so temperate."

"What else?" she asked. She suspected that family must be important to him. That was at odds with what she usually encountered in type-A, driven business executives, but then Justin didn't exactly fit the mold of what she expected from guys to begin with.

"Why are you really here?" she asked as they stepped out into the warm early-evening.

"I told you I like to know my opponents," he said.

"I can see that," she said. She did as well. Normally when she was negotiating something for her company she spent a lot of time researching the players involved in the deal. Winning almost always came down to who had the most information. "You were trying to throw me off my game a little, right?"

"In part," he admitted. "But honestly, you aren't what I was expecting from the Gonzalezes' lawyer."

"Because I'm a girl?" she asked using his term. "You know that calling me a girl wasn't exactly flattering?"

"I didn't mean it that way," he said. "It's because you're so sexy. I can handle going up against a girl but when she is making me think of long, hot nights instead of business—well I figured turnabout was fair play and I should do something unexpected like ask you out."

She bit her lower lip. He was a very frank man, which shouldn't surprise her. From the moment they'd met he'd been that way. He was the kind of man who shot from the hip and didn't worry about the consequences.

And she was a woman who'd been damned by the consequences of her reckless heart before. She had to remember that her grandparents were in this situation with the Luna Azul Company specifically because she'd followed her heart and they had paid the price.

"I'm not looking for a relationship," she said. "I am focused on my career."

"I can see that," he said. "But unless you're into lying to yourself, you'll admit that there is something between us."

She could admit that. There was a powerful attraction between them. Something that was more intense than anything she'd ever experienced before. She wanted to blame it on Miami and her old self, but she knew that it was Justin. If she'd been here with any other man she wouldn't have felt like this.

That was enough to make her pause. Justin was different and that very difference was enough to make him dangerous.

"Lust," she said. "And that is nothing more than a chimera."

"An illusion? I don't think so. Lust is our primal instincts telling us to pay attention. You could be a potential mate for me," he said.

She stopped walking on the wooden boardwalk and turned to face him. He'd put on a pair of aviator-style sunglasses and with his jacket slung over his shoulder he looked like he'd stepped off a yacht. He seemed like a man who was used to getting everything he wanted.

"What?" she asked. "There is no way you and I could

ever be mates. I just don't know if I should believe you or not. You're not really looking for a mate for more than one night, right?"

"Usually, I'd say so, but the way I am reacting to you throws my normal playbook out the window."

She shook her head. "Your playbook? Any guy who has one of those isn't someone I'm interested in."

"That sounded worse than I meant it to. I was trying to say that this attraction I feel for you is making me forget every rule I have about mixing business and pleasure."

"I can't afford to take a chance like that with you, Justin."

"Because of Tomas?"

She wished it were that simple. "If it didn't involve my grandparents…"

"What do you mean?" he asked.

She had no idea. She wished she had some answers. "Say I met you on vacation, I'd jump into a fling with you. But this is my home and my family and I can't afford to compromise anything."

"There is no need to compromise anything," Justin said, putting his hand in the center of her back and urging her to start walking again.

She shook her head and the scent of gardenias surrounded him. He closed his eyes and breathed deeply. Why was it that everything about Selena was a turn-on for him? "I'm not going to take no for an answer. We are both good at negotiating."

"This isn't easy for me. My grandparents deserve my undivided attention, I owe them," she said.

"Why do you owe them?" he asked. He wanted to know more about what had happened ten years ago and he was determined to get some answers, but not right now.

"I just do."

He nodded. "Well, I owe my brothers, and my company deserves my undivided attention, but I can't think of business when I'm with you. Right now all I can think of is your mouth and how it will feel under mine."

"Saying things like that is not helping me," she said, closing her eyes and wrapping her arms around her own waist.

If he pushed a little bit harder he could have her. He knew that. But he didn't want to crumble her defenses. He pulled her closer to him and moved them off the path out of the way of other walkers. "Have you thought about it?"

She nibbled on her full lower lip as she looked up at him. "I have, but I'm not about to play into your hands so easily."

He lowered his head, wanting to kiss her but at the same time wanting—no needing—her to want it too. He wanted her to be so attracted to him that she forgot her rules and her fears and everything else just faded away.

"Justin, stop manipulating me."

"I'm not," he said. "I want to see what it will take for you to forget about business and just see me as a man."

"Stop trying to play me," she said. "Just be yourself."

"I don't think you'd trust me," he said.

"I don't trust you now," she said. "And that feeling that you are toying with me is never going to help your case. I do want you but I don't want to be your pawn."

Her honesty cut straight through him. He really didn't

want her to be his pawn. He wanted her to be his woman. That was it.

He needed Selena no matter what the circumstances. And he was going to do whatever he had to to make that happen. He couldn't just walk away.

"I'm sorry. I was trying—"

"I know what you were trying to do," she said, lifting one hand and tracing the line of his lips. "I can understand it because I don't want to end up the weak one either."

He could hardly think when she touched him. He slid his hands together at her waist and pulled her more closely into his body.

He rubbed his lips against hers briefly and then stepped back before he gave in to temptation and ravished her mouth.

"We need…to walk," he said.

He took her hand with his and led her down the path. She laughed softly and he knew she was very aware of his desire. That didn't bother him at all. He wanted her to be very aware of him as a man and he knew that he'd accomplished that.

"We can't walk away from this," he said.

"I know," she admitted. "But I won't let this kind of attraction take control of my life."

He understood that. As a man, part of him was glad to hear that she wanted him that powerfully. The other part, the businessman who never took a day off, was glad to hear it, too, because it meant that he had the potential to use that attraction to get what he wanted.

Walking took the edge off her and allowed him to start thinking of something other than lifting her skirt and finding the sweetness between her legs. "What if we pretend you are on vacation?"

"Why?"

"Then it's like you said, we're just two people who are attracted to each other."

"Like a vacation fling?" she asked.

"Exactly like that. No talking about our families and their business interests. Just two people who've met and started an affair," he said.

"So it ends when I go back home?" she asked.

His gut said no. He didn't want to think about Selena leaving but he put that down to the fact that she was new to him. "If that is what we both decide, then yes."

She pulled her hand from his, stopped walking and turned to look out at the ocean. She wrapped one arm around her waist and he wondered if he'd ever know her well enough to know what she was thinking.

"I wish it could be that simple," she said, "But we both know there is no way we're going to be able—"

"I'm not someone who takes no for an answer," he said.

She glanced over her shoulder at him and he saw that fiery spark was back in her eyes. This couldn't be more than a fling and he wanted to keep it light. But the only way he was going to be able to deal with her in the boardroom was if he had her in his bedroom.

"I'm not going to let you bully me into making a decision like this."

"Is that what I'm doing or is that what you are telling yourself?"

She turned to face him full-on and walked over to him, hips swaying with each step. His mind went blank and suddenly he didn't care why she agreed but only that she did. He needed her to be one hundred percent his. And nothing was going to stand in the way of that. Not business and not even the lady herself. He knew that Selena Gonzalez wanted him and now he just had to find the right button to push, to convince her that she was willing to take a chance on him.

"I know my own mind, Justin Stern," she said as she closed the gap between them. She put her hands on his shoulders and tipped her head back to look up at him. "And I know exactly what I want."

She went up on her tiptoes, tunneled her fingers into his hair and planted a kiss on him that made him forget everything else. All he did was feel.

Her breasts cushioned against his chest. Her supple hips under his hands as he rested them there. Her soft hair brushing his cheek as she turned her head to angle her mouth better over his.

And then the thrust of her warm tongue into his mouth. How she slowly rubbed hers over his and then lifted her hands to his face to hold him right above the jaw. She kept his head steady as she tasted him and he let her.

Hell, there was no stopping this woman. She had turned his own game back on him and left him standing still. He drew his own hands up to her tiny waist and pulled her off balance into his body.

He sucked on her tongue when she would have pulled it back. Her hands slid down his neck to his shoulders and she moved her head again and a tiny moan escaped her.

His erection nudged the top of her thighs and he shifted his hips against hers and heard her moan again. This was more like it, he thought. This was the kind of negotiation he wanted. Both of them alone together.

Just man versus woman and let the winner take all.

Four

Selena had forgotten what it was like to turn the tables on a man sexually. She did it all the time at work but this was personal and she liked it. A heady mix of passion and power consumed her and she knew that it was well past time she got back in touch with this side of herself.

She'd given in to Justin not just because of the lust that was flowing between them but also because she needed to reclaim her femininity.

She took Justin's hand and led him back to the hotel. "Why are we wasting our time out here when we could be up in my room?"

"Your room? I thought you weren't sure about my proposition."

"I guess you think too much." Turning the tables on Justin had knocked him off balance and she knew he would be easier to deal with now. "I like the idea of a vacation fling. It's been too long for me and being with you…well let's just say you are the perfect distraction."

He frowned at her, but she didn't care. She wasn't stupid. She knew that even though Justin wanted her—she knew he wasn't faking his attraction to her—a part of him was focused on how to use the lust they both felt to his own advantage.

And she wasn't going to let him do that. She wanted him. She needed a distraction from being back here in Miami. She was thinking too much about the girl she had been and Justin was the distraction she needed.

"Come back to my room," she said, leaning closer and kissing his neck right under his ear. "That's what we'd do if we were on vacation."

Justin nodded. "But we aren't on vacation."

"Have you changed your mind?" she asked.

"No. But I don't like the way you changed yours. What's going on behind those beautiful brown eyes?" he asked.

She pulled back. She couldn't do this. It wasn't like her to just impulsively invite a man back to her room. He was right, what was she thinking?

"Nothing. Nothing is going on," she said. "I think I had a momentary fever but it is passing now."

She felt small and a bit rejected. She'd actually never been that bold with a man before. The dress and the way that Justin treated her had made her feel like she was sexy, an enchantress, and now she was realizing she was still just Selena.

"I think we should head back to the hotel. I need to freshen up before heading to dinner. I will meet you there."

She turned to walk away needing to get back to her

room. She needed to find someplace private to sit down and regroup.

"No."

She glanced over her shoulder at him.

"No?"

"That's what I said. I am not letting you run away," he said, taking her hand in his. "What's going on with you?"

She shook her head and swallowed hard. "I'm sorry. You are making me a little…crazy."

"That's good. That's what I was going for…trying to distract you," he admitted.

"Well, you did a good job tonight. But that won't affect me in the boardroom when we are meeting with your group and the community leaders."

"I didn't think it would. To be honest I'm trying to even the scales. You have me thinking about your curvy body and kissing you instead of business and I wanted you to think of me."

"Does that mean you don't really want a vacation fling with me?"

"Hell, no. I want you more than I want my next breath. But I want you to want it for the right reasons—not because you think it will help you in the boardroom. I do believe we can keep this attraction between us private and explore it."

She thought about what he was saying. She wanted him and she wasn't going to deny it. "I'm not—Miami is more than just my home. It's the place that shaped me into the woman I am today and coming back here is stirring up all kinds of things in me I didn't expect."

"Like what?" he asked.

Justin was dangerous, she thought. He made her feel

so comfortable and safe that she would tell him almost anything. "This dress for one thing. I bought this for you."

"I like it."

"That was my intention, but at home…in Manhattan I'd never wear this."

"Good," he said, leading them back toward the hotel. "Be yourself with me, Selena. I want to see that woman you keep tucked away from the rest of the world. I don't want to be like every other guy to you."

"There is no way you could be. My family told me you're the devil."

He laughed. It was a strong masculine sound and it made her smile. "I haven't been called the devil before."

"To your face," she said.

"Touché," he said as they reached the hotel and stepped into the air-conditioned lobby.

Chills spread down her arms and she shivered just a bit. "Are we okay now?" he asked.

"I think so," she said. "I will meet you—"

"Get whatever you need. I want to take you to Luna Azul."

"Why?"

"I want to show you my family," he said.

"After," she said. "I need some time to myself before we go to dinner at my grandparents."

"Really? I was hoping you'd go with me. I don't want to walk in there by myself."

"Since when does the devil show fear?" she asked.

"I have no idea, since I'm not the devil," he said.

"What are you?" she asked.

"Just a man who likes a pretty girl and doesn't want to screw up again."

Selena watched him walk away, wondering if she'd underestimated him and if that would be at her own peril.

Justin sat quietly in his car parked on the street in front of the Gonzalez home. Selena had withdrawn into herself and there had been no drawing her out. He had a feeling that Selena's attitude was the least of his problems as he got out and walked up the driveway to the house.

There was music coming from the backyard and the delicious smells of charcoal and roasting meat wafted around him. This was a cozy neighborhood, the kind of place where he could buy two or three houses and not feel the sting in his checkbook, but a place where he'd never fit in.

Was this what Selena had been talking about when she said Luna Azul didn't belong in Little Havana?

"*Amigo,* you coming?"

The guy who walked by him was in his early twenties with close-cut dark hair and warm olive-colored skin. He wasn't as tall as Justin and his face was friendly.

"I am indeed," Justin said. He had a six-pack of Landshark beer in one hand and some flowers for Selena's grandmother.

"How do you know Tomas?" the young man asked.

"We're in business together." Justin wasn't about to pretend he had any other reason to be here. In fact, in light of his drinks with Selena he thought wooing her was going about as smoothly as the entire buying-the-marketplace deal. What was it with the Gonzalez family? Was it impossible to find a common path with them?

"Truly? My *abuelito* usually doesn't do business with...wait a minute, are you Justin Stern?"

"That's me," he said. Great, nice to know that he already had a reputation here and he hadn't even arrived yet.

"Oh, ho, you have some guts showing up here," the kid said.

"I was invited, and I'm not a bad guy," Justin told him. "I am trying to find a way to make that market viable, not to run your grandparents out."

The kid tipped his head to the side, studying him. "I'm watching you."

"I'm glad. Family should look out for one another. And I'm not going to take advantage of your grandparents or your family. My main concern is making money from the property we bought."

"Is money all you care about?"

Justin shook his head. He saw Selena walking up toward the house from where they stood in the shade of a large palm tree. She'd changed from the sexy dress she had worn earlier into a pair of khaki walking shorts and a sleeveless wraparound top. She was enchanting, he thought.

He forgot about how unwelcome this guy was making him feel and focused on Selena.

"Leave him alone, Enrique. He's not a bad guy," Selena said as she came up to them.

"He told me the same thing," Enrique said. "Are you sure about him?"

Selena shrugged. "Not one hundred percent but I'm getting there."

"If we do business with your family," Enrique said, turning to Justin, "I want to talk to you about deejaying at Luna Azul. Why do you only hire New York and LA deejays?"

Justin had very little to do with the everyday running

of the nightclub he owned with his brothers. "I don't have an answer for that but I can find out. If you send me a demo tape—"

"I don't think Enrique wants to work for you," Selena said.

"I'll make my own decisions, *tata,*" Enrique said. He reached around Justin and hugged her. She hugged him back.

"Enrique is my little brother," she said.

"I'm taller than you now, sis. I think that makes me your 'big' little brother," Enrique said with a grin that was familiar to Justin. He'd seen it on Selena's face a few times.

"You'll always be my baby brother," she said, looping her arm through Enrique's and Justin was relegated to following the two siblings up the walk to the house.

Justin had the feeling he'd always be an outsider. Too bad his little brother wasn't here tonight. This was exactly the type of party that Nate was better at than he was.

But he was here to achieve two things: first, to have Tomas lift the injunction against Luna Azul and second, to get Selena to be that warm, seductive woman she'd been on the beach again.

He'd pulled back for her sake, had instinctively known that she wasn't the kind of woman who could start an affair, even a short-term one, with a man she barely knew.

But tonight he'd change all of that. He slipped his arm through Selena's free one and she hesitated and lost her footing, glancing up at him.

"What are you doing?"

"Just making sure everyone knows who invited me to the party."

Enrique laughed. "No one's going to doubt that, bro. This is Selena's welcome-home party. Did you know she hasn't been back here since my tenth birthday?"

Why not? "No, I didn't know that. I'm honored to have been invited to this party then."

"Don't forget that," Enrique said. He dropped Selena's arm to open the front door of the house. The air-conditioned coolness rushed out and the sounds of the party filled the lanai.

"Enrique's in the house," Enrique yelled and there was a round of applause.

Selena took a deep breath. "I am not sure this was my best idea."

"I am. I want to get to know your family."

She paused there on the step so that they were almost eye level. "Why? So you can use it to your advantage?"

"No, so I can start to understand you."

He put his hand on the small of her back and directed her into the living room. Everyone surrounded her and welcomed her home. But standing to the side, Justin realized that Selena hesitated to be a part of them. She held a part of herself back and he wanted to know why.

Selena was amazed to see Justin actually fitting in with her family. He was standing by the grill talking to the men about baseball of all things. But then she guessed he would know a little bit about the sport thanks to his brother, the former ball player.

"What's the matter, *tata?* Aren't you enjoying your party?"

Her grandmother sat down beside her and put her arm around Selena's shoulders. For just a minute she felt like she was twelve again and a hug from this woman could solve all of her problems. She put her head on her grandmother's shoulder and just sat there enjoying the scent of gardenia perfume and how safe she felt at this moment.

"No, I'm not. I feel like everyone is watching me," Selena said.

"They are. We have missed you so much since you left."

"I don't want everyone to remember what happened. I'm sorry, *abuelita*. Did I ever tell you how sorry I was?"

Her grandmother tucked a strand of Selena's hair behind her ear and kissed her lightly on the cheek. "You did. Stop living in the past, that's all done and we are better for it."

"Better? If it wasn't for me you wouldn't be in this position with Justin Stern."

"And you wouldn't have met him. I've noticed you watching Mr. Stern."

Selena blushed. "Given my track record with men, that should alarm you, *abuelita,* not make you smile."

Her grandmother laughed. "The heart doesn't care about the same things as the brain. My own sister Dona was in love with a gringo and our papa forbid her from seeing him and do you know what she did?"

"She ran away and married him and they lived happily ever after. Even reconciling with the family eventually," Selena said. She'd heard this story many times but for the first time she understood what her grandmother had been trying to say to her. "Why would Aunt Dona do that? I mean living away from the family is hard."

"She wasn't on her own, *tata,* not like you in New York. That's why I think everything has happened for a reason. A man drove you away from your family and this man," she said, gesturing to Justin, "has brought you back to us regardless of his intention."

"I'm not sure I'm ready to see Justin as a white knight."

"He is cute, though."

"*Abuelita,* I'm not sure you should be noticing that."

"Why not? It's not like I said he has a nice butt," she added with a wink.

"But he does have one, doesn't he?" Selena agreed and then blushed, remembering the way the rest of his body had felt pressed to hers.

"He sure does."

"*Abuelita,* what would *abuelito* say if he heard you talking like that?"

"He knows where my heart lies," she said. "Can I say something to you, *tata?*"

"Of course."

"You have never known where your heart lies," she said. "You were always fixated on getting out of here and doing bigger and better things, but I don't think you understood the true cost."

There was truth there. Truth that Selena had never wanted to acknowledge before and she knew that it was time to. Maybe it was because she was thirty now and had made enough mistakes in her life to have really experienced the ups and downs in life. "I think you are right."

"I know I am," her grandmother said with a laugh. "Are you thirsty? I need another mojito."

"Did I hear my lady ask for a mojito?" Tomas asked coming over to them.

Her grandmother stood up and kissed her grandfather. "Yes, you did."

Selena watched them together and felt a pang in her heart. Her own parents had married young and filled their house with love and laughter and a few tears when it took so long for her mother to have a second child. She wanted what those couples had. That was her destiny. Though she loved her job and her apartment in Manhattan.

"Come and dance with your grandfather," Tomas said, drawing her to her feet.

"Wouldn't you rather dance with *abuelita?*"

"I will dance with her later. Right now I want to dance with my beautiful granddaughter. I'm so happy you've come home, *tata.*"

Enrique was playing music with a strong Latin beat, mixing the contemporary artists with the old ones her grandfather and his brothers liked. The song playing was a samba and she danced with her grandfather, forgetting all of her troubles and her worries. Laughing with her cousins and aunts and uncles over missteps and bumping hips.

She closed her eyes and for a second allowed herself some self-forgiveness and enjoyed being back in the best home she'd ever found. She enjoyed the smile on her grandfather's face and the way her little brother looked as he spun the music and watched their family.

Her family.

Her eyes met Justin's and she felt a pulsing start in the very core of her body and move up and over her. She wanted that man. But she could never have Justin and have her family, too. Because no matter what he might say, his objective was always going to be money and hers had to be the heart of this family and the community they lived in.

She turned away from him. She wished she were the big-city woman she'd thought she was. Someone who could have a short-term affair that was about nothing but sex. But a big part of her wasn't sure that she could. She was still the sheltered Latina she'd always been. And being back here she felt more that woman than ever before.

She wanted more from Justin Stern than just sex. And he could never give her that.

Five

Justin liked Selena's cousins, Paulo and Jorge. They made him laugh and he understood them because they were both successful businessmen who were used to doing what they had to to get the job done. If only Tomas were a little more like his grandsons, then Justin had the feeling he wouldn't be facing an injunction.

"I'd love to have you on a committee I'm putting together to make sure that the renovation of the Cuban American marketplace is both profitable and a benefit to Little Havana."

"I'll think about it. But my plate is pretty full," Jorge said.

"I'll do it," Paulo said. "We need new investors to come here and I really like what you've done with Luna Azul. That's the kind of club we need down here. And it drives business to my restaurant."

"That's the kind of synergy I think we can have at the marketplace."

"You should call it a Mercado instead of marketplace," Selena said coming over to join them.

"She's right," Jorge said. "I think you should have a Latin music store there. My boys have to drive across town to find the music and instruments they need. And you could tie it to the bands that play at Luna Azul… have them stop in there for a release party or a little concert."

"I like that idea," Justin said. But discussing business while Selena was standing so close that she was pressed against his arm wasn't conducive. He could barely think since all of the blood in his body was racing to his groin and not his brain.

"Did you invite them to be on the community committee?"

"I did," he said.

"Good, so you are done talking business?"

"No," Justin said.

"He's like us, *tata,* he'll be dead and buried before he stops trying to make a deal," Paulo said.

Justin laughed and Selena smiled but he could tell that her cousin's words disturbed her. A few minutes later the food was ready and the other men moved to prepare the platters for everyone to eat. He took Selena's arm and drew her away from the crowd.

"Why does what Paulo said bother you?" he asked her.

"It just reaffirmed my fears that you are attracted to me because it might make dealing with my family easier," she said.

That was blunt and honest and he shouldn't have been

surprised, since Selena wasn't the kind of woman who was tentative about anything.

"I want you," he said. "That's it, end of story. If you said to me right now that you were going to keep that injunction in place against my company until we both died, it wouldn't change a thing. I still want you naked and writhing against me."

"Lust."

"We discussed that."

"I know. And I thought I'd found a solution."

"Vacation fling," he said.

"It's the only way to keep this in perspective," she said.

He understood where she was coming from. He'd watched his own father love a woman who didn't want him. Not the way he wanted her. It had always been Justin's fear in relationships. He knew that if he ever fell in love it would dull his razor-sharp edge when it came to business. And he'd been careful to make lust his criterion for a relationship. Never really getting to know the family or friends of the women he slept with.

"I'm not going to lie to you, Selena. I will use whatever means necessary to make that marketplace successful, but that will not change how I feel about you. And I always go after what I want."

"I bet you get it, too," she said.

"Yes, I do. Today has been eye-opening for me."

"Because of that dress I wore earlier?" she asked.

"Partly. I don't think I've recovered full brain function since then."

She laughed. "It's nice to know I have a little power over you."

"You have more than you know. Inviting me here was

a very well-played move on your part. Talking to your cousins made me realize that we should be reaching out here more than we do. Luna Azul is successful in this location without community support. Imagine what we could do with support."

"I have imagined it. That's why it is important that my grandparents are in on the ground level."

"I see that. I can't wait to have the first committee meeting."

"Me, too," she said.

"Now about us," he said after a few minutes of silence had fallen between them.

"There isn't any *us*."

"Not yet," he said. "But we both want it, so it's silly to pretend that we don't."

"Vacation fling, right?"

"I'm open to suggestions," he said. "I don't want to forget that you have a life in another part of the country and that you will be going back there."

"That was a surprisingly honest thing for you to admit," she said.

"There is no reason for me to pretend that you don't have the potential to be a heartbreaker. I've never met another woman like you, Selena."

He was a shoot-from-the-hip kind of guy and he wasn't going to change at this late date. Especially where Selena was concerned. She needed to know that even though he was suggesting a vacation fling, he wanted it as badly as she did. He couldn't get her out of his mind and until he did he had the feeling he was going to be operating on backup power instead of at full strength.

Everyone filled their plates and sat down to eat, and though he knew these people thought he was their enemy, he felt like he could be part of this family. He wanted to be here not as a business rival, but as Selena's date.

After dinner was over, Selena mingled for the rest of the evening trying to stay as far from Justin as she could.

He'd waved at her earlier and said goodbye, but that was it. She tried not to be disappointed. After all that had been her one desire, right? She'd been tired of trying to avoid him and the attraction she felt for him. Now she could just be a granddaughter and a niece and a cousin and not have to answer uncomfortable questions about a man who was too good-looking and a point of conflict with her family.

"Why are you hiding out over here?" Enrique asked as he sat down next to her on the wrought-iron bench nestled between the hibiscus trees.

"I'm not hiding out," she said. "I'm just taking a break."

"From the family?" he asked. "I guess when you aren't used to it our kin can be a little overwhelming."

She had to agree. It had been so long since she'd been to a family gathering that she found it tiring and loud. And she wasn't sure she fit in here anymore.

"Are you used to it?" she asked him.

He shrugged. "It's all I know."

"Have you thought any more about coming to New York and living with me for a while?"

She wanted her baby brother to see more of the world than just this slice of it but so far he'd resisted her efforts to bring him up north to the city.

"I have, *tata,* but I don't think I will do it. I like Miami and the family and everything. And I don't want to move away from here."

She nodded. She understood where Enrique was coming from. When she'd left home, she'd felt she had to and those first few years had been terrifying. She'd hated being away from everything familiar. That first October had felt so cold and she'd almost come back home; only shame had kept her in New York. Only slowly had she shed the girl she'd once been and become the woman she was today.

"It's an open invitation."

"I know it is, sis. How'd you like my music?"

"I loved it. You are a talented deejay."

"I know," he said with an arrogant grin. "I'm going to use Justin Stern to get a gig at Luna Azul."

"How is that going to work? He's not an easy man to use," she said. She didn't want her brother and Justin spending too much time together.

"He wants something from us and I will offer to help him get it if he helps me."

Her brother was always working an angle. "Be careful. Justin isn't the kind of guy who gives up things easily."

"I can tell that. But I think with the right manipulation it could work."

"Let me know if I can help. He's putting together a committee to discuss his marketplace. Perhaps you can get a gig at the ground-breaking if we reach an arrangement with his company."

"Great! I like that idea, *tata*."

She hugged him close. "I knew you would."

She missed Enrique probably the most of all the people she'd left behind. He'd only been ten when she'd left. It had been just a year after their parents had died and she knew she should have stayed to help in raising him but she'd been too young to do that. And after Raul and the con he'd run on her family, she'd had to get away and prove herself.

"I wish you'd move back here, *tata*."

"I can't."

He nodded. "A group of us are going clubbing, you want to join?"

"Who?"

"The cousins. Some of them are older than you."

"Geez, thanks."

"You know what I mean," Enrique said. "It will be fun. And it's not like you have to be at work tomorrow."

"That's true. I'm on vacation—sort of," she said, thinking back to earlier when Justin had offered to be her vacation fling. Was she overthinking this?

"You are on vacation. Come on, live a little."

She nodded. "I'd like that. Am I dressed okay?"

"You're perfect," Enrique said. "Hey, guys, Selena is coming with us."

"Great, let's go."

She followed Enrique over to Jorge and Paulo and a group of her other cousins. The tiki torches that had been placed around the edge of the yard still burned and there were plates and cups littering every surface.

"I have to help clean up first," she said. Her grandparents didn't need to be doing all this work by themselves.

"No, you don't," her grandmother said as she came up behind her and wrapped an arm around her waist. "Go and have some fun with your cousins. Remember what it's like to have family around you."

"*Abuelita,* I always remember that."

"Then I hope you also know that we love you. I will call you in the morning," her grandmother said.

"I'm not staying at my house, *abuelita*."

"Where are you staying then?"

"At the Ritz. Call me on my cell phone, okay?"

"*Tata...*"

"I just couldn't stay there. I hope you aren't upset."

"I'm not upset, but I worry about you."

"The hotel is nice and I can relax there," Selena said.

Her grandmother hugged her. "Then that is all that matters."

"Whatever you do, don't call too early, *abuelita*," Jorge said. "We are going to be partying all night. It's not too often the prodigal daughter returns home."

Selena shook her head. "I'm not the prodigal anything."

Jorge put his arm around her as they walked through the house. He and she had been so close growing up. Their mothers were twins and the two of them had been born only eight days apart. Jorge was more than a cousin to her. He was her big brother and her childhood twin.

"That's the sad part, *tata,* you don't even realize how important you are to us all and how much we've all missed you."

"But I am responsible for ruining—"

"You aren't responsible for anything but the actions you took to make things right. And you did make up for everything that happened long ago. Stop punishing yourself for it," Jorge said.

"I'm not punishing myself."

"Yes, you are. And it's time you stopped."

* * *

Nate and Cam weren't pleased with the news that they'd have to wait on the ground-breaking. Actually, Nate didn't seem to care too much but Cam was ready to use every contact he had to make the Gonzalez family suffer.

"We can't do that," Justin said as he sipped his Landshark beer and relaxed in the VIP area of the rooftop club at Luna Azul.

"I know but it would make me feel good. Tell me what you have planned."

"I'm taking the zoning commissioner out for some golf, which should help to speed up the review process. We haven't broken any laws and I've reviewed the injunction they filed against us."

"Are we in the right?"

"We haven't done anything yet so technically we're fine. There is a zoning provision to keep the marketplace as part of the community. I think this committee will satisfy that."

"Good. Then there's no problem?"

"Cam, bureaucracy runs slowly. And you want everything finished yesterday. We are going to be lucky to have a ground-breaking at the tenth anniversary party."

Nate shook his head. "Cam, are you going to stand for that defeatist attitude?"

"Shut up, little bro," Justin said. "We have to be realistic."

"I don't have to be," Cam said. "I have you to do that. I think I will be on the committee with you and we will get as many local business owners involved with the anniversary celebration as we can. Once they have a vested interest in the celebration they will help make things happen."

"I agree," Justin said. "I have a young deejay who I can get to play at the marketplace ground-breaking—he is Tomas Gonzalez's grandson."

Cam nodded over at him. "You're already taking steps to make this happen. Keep us updated on your progress."

"I will. How's everything else going at the club? Do you need anything from me?" Justin asked.

"Just get the approvals for that ground-breaking taken care of, we can handle the rest," Nate said.

"I will. I'm going to take a few days for a staycation," Justin said.

"What? You can't take any time off," Cam said. "Not now."

"I guess I'm explaining this wrong. I'll be working every day but at night I'm going to be staying at the Ritz," Justin said.

"Why?" Nate asked. "I mean the Ritz is nice but why not stay at your home?"

There was no way he was going to tell his brothers that this move involved a woman. "I just haven't had a break lately and staying at the Ritz will give me one."

"As long as you are still working, it doesn't matter to me," Cam said.

"I might have you check in on some friends who are staying down there," Nate said.

"I don't want to have to check in on your celebs."

Nate ran with the celebrity crowd—all friends he'd made back when he'd been a major league baseball player. And Nate still used these connections for the club, even though he was recently engaged to Jen Miller, a dance instructor at Luna Azul. They were a cute couple and very happy together. Justin was surprised that his playboy brother had fallen for the pretty dancer and her quiet lifestyle.

While Justin was glad his younger brother had kept in contact with the glitter set, the last thing he wanted was to have to socialize with them.

For the most part he had nothing in common with people who traded on their looks or talent to get by in the world. He'd always used hard work and determination.

"Fine. We can have drinks tomorrow night when I'm down there."

"Why do we have to?" Justin asked just to needle his brother.

"Because you are making me drive down there. And you're buying!" Nate said as his cell phone rang. He glanced at the screen and then excused himself.

Warm breezes blew across the rooftop patio. "I like this place," Justin said.

Cam arched one eyebrow at him. "I'm glad to hear it, considering you helped me build it."

Justin nodded. "I know. I wonder how different it could have been if we had real community support?"

Cam took a sip of his whiskey and then rubbed the back of his neck. "In the early days it would have made a big difference. I hate to think of what it was like before Nate got injured and came home...do you remember that first summer when he just sat in the back of the club and his baseball playing friends visited?"

"Yes. You wanted to turn the club that we'd invested every last penny in, into a sports bar."

"Hey, it seemed like a good idea at the time," Cam said.

"It was a good idea, I'm just glad we didn't have to do

it. By the way, Selena suggested calling the marketplace the Mercado. I like it."

"Yes, I like it, too. Who is Selena?"

Justin took a deep breath. It didn't matter that he and Cam held equal positions of authority in the company; Cam was always going to be Justin's big brother. "She's the lawyer the Gonzalezes hired. She's also their grand-daughter."

"Pretty?"

"Breathtakingly beautiful," Justin admitted.

"Can you still be objective? If not, we can use one of your junior managers to take the lead on this."

"No," Justin said. "I've got this under control."

"Is she staying at the Ritz?"

Justin just nodded.

"I'm not sure how under control you have this," Cam said.

"I'm not going to let you down or do anything to hurt the Luna Azul."

"I know that," Cam said. "What about yourself? Are you going to do anything to harm *you?*"

Justin finished his drink with a long, hard swallow and then got to his feet. "I'm the Tin Man, Cam. No heart. So nothing to be hurt by Selena."

Justin walked away from his brother and wished that it wasn't true. But he had learned a long time ago that women and love never really touched him on a deep level. True, this attraction to Selena was intense but it would burn out like all things did.

Six

Justin walked through his house, pausing beneath the portrait of his family that had been done when Cam graduated high school. They looked like the perfect family. Picture-perfect, he thought. On the outside they'd always made sure to present a front that others would envy.

And what a front it was. His father, the pro golfer, who traveled to tournaments in his private jet, and their socialite mother, who moved in all the right circles and made sure that her sons were successful and dated the right kind of girls.

He glanced up at his mother, really staring at the blonde woman with her perfectly coiffed hair, and wondered why she'd never been happy with their family. No matter how well he did in school or how well Nate had played baseball, she'd never been pleased with them.

She'd never smiled or shown them any real signs of love or affection.

He'd often thought that all women were that way but he'd seen his brother fall in love with Jen and therefore got to see a different side to women. Jen had cracked through Nate's doubts. Justin was still a bit cynical but seeing how Jen and Nate had worked together to make their relationship successful...well, it made him wonder why his mom hadn't tried just a little bit harder to make it work with his dad.

"Mr. Stern?"

He glanced over his shoulder and saw his butler standing there. "Yes, Frank?"

"I have your bags ready. Do you want me to drive you to the Ritz?"

"No. I'm going to take the Porsche."

"I will park it in the circle drive. Do you need anything from me?"

"No. You can take the next two weeks off."

"Thank you, sir, but I don't have anywhere to go," Frank said.

Justin knew that Frank was always at work and he appreciated it. "Don't you have any family?"

"Not really. I left them behind a long time ago. I could go to Vegas but I really don't like to go more than once a year."

Justin smiled at his butler. Frank was a very carefully measured man. He didn't want to give in to his enjoyment of gambling and let it become an addiction. Frank would only go to Vegas and only once a year.

"I get that."

"Can I ask you a question, sir?"

"Go ahead."

"Why are you going to the Ritz? You have a better place here."

Frank was making perfect sense, logically speaking. "I am...let's just say there is a woman at the Ritz."

"And you want to be closer to her? I think you should invite her here," Frank said.

"That would make things a lot more complicated."

"I guess it would," Frank said.

It probably still didn't make sense, but Frank was his employee and was never going to tell him he was barking mad, even if that was what he thought. Frank was good at holding his tongue. "Frank, sometimes I think I don't pay you enough!"

"I agree, sir," Frank said. "I'll bring the car and get your bags in it."

"Thank you, Frank."

"Just doing my job, sir."

"I appreciate it," Justin said. Frank left and Justin moved away from the portrait.

Was he making the right decision or was he just going to come off as a stalker? If he and Selena were going to have a vacation fling it would make sense for them to both be at the hotel. That's how vacation flings happened.

He knew from experience. He liked the anonymity that being at the hotel would afford them. If he brought her to his home, she'd see his family and his neighbors and it would make their fling seem more real.

And when she left to go back to New York he'd have memories of her in his space. He didn't want that. He wanted their relationship to be uncomplicated. To be a true fling. One where neither of them got hurt.

He wasn't going to pretend that she didn't have the potential to hurt him. He had no idea what the outcome would be of an affair with her but he couldn't resist the thought of having her in his arms.

He wanted her.

That was the bottom line and he was going to do whatever he had to in order to get her. He didn't care if he had to pay the cost later.

All around him were the trappings of success and that made him even more determined to ensure that this thing with Selena worked out. He wasn't used to failing and he wouldn't this time. Selena was the first thing he wanted just for himself.

Selena was buzzed and hot and had forgotten the last time she'd had this much fun. Clubbing wasn't her thing. To be honest it never had been. She'd always been a very studious girl and when she'd met Raul he'd kept her isolated from others. Part of the reason his con had worked so well.

But tonight she didn't want to think about any of that. Jorge came out of the club and sat down next to her on the bench. "Are you hiding out?"

"No. Cooling down. I haven't danced that much in years," she admitted.

"What do you do for fun in New York?" he asked.

"Nothing. I don't have fun. I just work and go home."

"All work and no play makes for one big boring life, *tata*."

"It didn't seem so bad until tonight," she admitted. "It's a quiet life but also an uncomplicated one."

Jorge put his arm along the back of the bench and hugged her to his side. "You need to relax."

"I think you are right. Tonight was a lot of fun. I

never guessed that just dancing would be so liberating. I forgot about everything when I was out there."

Jorge smiled at her. His grin reminded her of her father's and she felt a pang in her heart. She missed her parents so much.

"That's the point of clubbing. I think we will have to take you out again."

"I might let you," she said. "But I'm worn out now. I am going to call a cab to take me back to my hotel."

"Hotel? Why aren't you staying at your old house?" Jorge asked.

"Too many memories," she said.

He nodded. "Why haven't you sold that place?"

She shrugged. "I sometimes get income from renting it and I give that money to *abuelito*. It's the least I can do."

"*Tata,* you have to let go of the past or you are always going to be stuck in it," Jorge said.

"I did let go, remember? I live in New York," she said.

"That wasn't letting go, that was running away," Jorge said. "You are punishing yourself by staying away. No one in the family blames you for what happened. You need to forgive yourself."

"That is easier said than done," she said.

"Don't I know it," he said.

"How do you know that?" she asked.

"I had an affair last year. Carina took me back and she says she's forgiven me, but I don't think I will ever feel worthy of her again."

"Carina is a nicer person than I am," Selena said. "I would never…"

"I thought so, too. But what I have with her is worth

fighting for. I had no idea how much I loved that woman until I thought I'd lost her forever."

"Love is so complicated," Selena said. Raul had been able to manipulate her because she'd been totally in love with him. Other people had told her he wasn't the perfect angel she'd believed him to be but that hadn't mattered. In her mind and in her heart she'd made excuses for him. She didn't want to do the same with Justin.

"Yes it is," Jorge said. "But there is nothing else like it on earth. I wouldn't trade my feelings for Carina for anything."

"Did I hear my name?" Carina asked, coming out to join them. "I wondered where you got to."

"Just visiting with Selena. I don't think she knows how much we all miss her."

"We do all miss you," Carina said. She looked over at Jorge, and Selena had the impression that Carina still wasn't sure of her man. She might have forgiven her husband, but it was clear that she hadn't relearned how to trust him.

"I'm calling a cab," Selena said.

"No, don't," Jorge said. "We will take you home. I'm ready to be alone with my woman."

Carina closed her eyes as Jorge hugged her close and it was almost painful to watch them together now that Selena knew their secret. She wondered if all couples had a secret. Something that bound them together and made them stronger. And she did believe her cousin and his wife would be stronger once Carina knew that Jorge was sincere. But that would take some time.

Jorge went in to tell the rest of her cousins that they were leaving.

"Tonight was fun," Selena said.

"Yes, it was. It's not really my scene—I like to stay

at home, but Jorge likes to hit the clubs and we have worked out a compromise where we will do it once a month," Carina said.

"Does that work?" Selena asked.

"It does. I actually like going out with him. It's not the way I thought it would be. And Jorge has agreed to take ballroom dancing classes with me."

Selena couldn't see her cousin doing ballroom dancing, but if it made Carina happy, she guessed that he would do it. "Where do you take lessons?"

"At Luna Azul. Jen Miller, who teaches their Latin dance classes, also knows ballroom and she is showing us a few moves."

"Do you think Luna Azul has been good for the neighborhood?" Selena asked her, her head clearing from the mojitos she'd been drinking all night.

"I do. They have captured the feel of old Havana in the club. My papa won't admit it to his friends but he likes going there because it reminds him of the stories his *abuelito* used to tell of pre-Castro Havana."

"I need to check it out and learn a bit about the enemy."

"I think you will be surprised by how much it fits given that they are outsiders."

Jorge came out of the club and they left. During the ride, Selena sat quietly in the backseat of the Dodge Charger. She thought about Justin Stern and dancing with him. She had a feeling that he'd claim to be an awkward dancer, but prove to be very efficient at it.

She closed her eyes and thought about the night and what she'd learned. She'd almost made a costly emotional mistake when she'd asked Justin up to her room. But living at the hotel was giving her the distance she needed from her family and tomorrow she'd figure out how to start a fling with Justin. Flirting with him earlier and dancing tonight had stirred her blood. She wanted Justin Stern and she wasn't going to deny herself.

Justin checked in and got settled in his hotel room. He'd left a voice mail for Selena. He was surprised she was out so late. It was almost midnight. Where was she?

He didn't like the tight feeling in his chest or the anger he felt at not knowing where she was. They were nothing but business rivals to each other. Nothing more than that. He'd have to remember that fact.

He paced around his room like a caged tiger. She was probably with another man. Why shouldn't she be? There wasn't another man in this city who was bringing as many complications to the table as he was. Not one. And he knew it.

She was the last woman he should be this obsessed with but the truth was he did want her. And he should never have let her go when he'd had her in his arms earlier.

The only time they were going to be this unaware of the complications of hooking up was right now. Before they got to know each other better. That was how things like this worked.

He didn't think about it anymore but just walked out of his room. He needed a walk to clear his head.

The elevator opened as he was standing there and Selena got off the car.

"What are you doing here?" they said at the same time.

"I'm staying here," she said.

"So am I."

"Why?" she asked. "And how did you get on my floor. That is almost stalkerish."

"I'm not stalking you. I had no idea this was the floor you were on. I asked for a suite."

"Okay, fine. But why are you here?"

"If we are going to have a vacation affair, we both should be on vacation."

She tipped her head to the side. "I guess that makes a little sense. But...I liked staying here where no one knew me."

"We just met," he pointed out.

"That's true but you are already trying to worm your way under my defenses."

"Worm? That isn't exactly flattering."

She smiled. "Good, it wasn't meant to be."

"Where have you been tonight?" he asked.

"Clubbing with my cousins. I've never been clubbing before," she said. "Have you ever gone?"

"Yes. I'm co-owner of a nightclub, remember?"

"That's right. You probably write it off on your taxes as research."

He did, but he didn't say so. "Did you dance with a lot of men?"

"Jealous?"

"Incredibly," he said, moving closer to her. She was leaning against the wall next to the elevator and he put his hands on either side of her head.

He leaned in closer until his lips brushed against hers. "Who did you dance with?"

"My cousins, my brother, but I dreamed it was you," she said with her eyes half-closed. "I don't think I should have told you that."

He felt that tight ball in his stomach relax. "You definitely should have told me."

He kissed her softly on the lips and she wrapped her arms around his neck.

"Are you a good dancer?" she asked as he broke the kiss.

"I don't know. No one has ever complained," he said.

"I knew you'd say something like that. Do you like holding me?" she asked.

He realized she was a little tipsy and saying things that she probably wouldn't have otherwise.

"I do. Do you like being in my arms?"

"Definitely. But you are just my vacation stud, remember that," she said to him.

"I won't forget it. Which room is yours?"

"Number 3106," she said. "Why?"

"I think we should get you to your room and out of the hallway."

"Good idea. I'm tired, Justin."

"I know, sweetie."

"Sweetie? Did you call me sweetie?"

"I did. Any objections?"

"No. I think I like it, but we're really not close enough for you to call me that."

"I wish we were," he said.

"Do you?"

"I wouldn't have said it if it weren't true."

"Are you a straight talker?" she asked.

"Sometimes. With you I am more than I want to be. You seem to bring out the awkward truth in me."

She giggled, and the sound enchanted him. She was such a sweet girl when her defenses were down. He helped her open her door and saw that her suite was laid out the reverse of his.

"I wanted you in my room earlier," she said.

"Not really," he said. "I think you were trying to throw me."

"I was," she admitted. "But a part of me did want you here. It's so much easier to start an affair before you have time to think of the risks involved."

"Yes, it is. But we aren't going to start one tonight," he said.

"We aren't? Why not?" she asked.

He leaned down and kissed her because he was human and a man who wanted her very much. The kiss was passionate and intense, all the things he'd known it would be, but at the same time the taste of those minty mojitos she'd been drinking all night lingered on her tongue. She wasn't herself tonight. And he wanted her to be fully aware of what she was doing when they did become lovers.

She wrapped her arms around his neck and tipped her head back to look up at him. "I like the way you feel in my arms."

"I do, too. I've never had a woman fit so well in my arms before. Your head nestles just right on my shoulder, your breasts are cushioned perfectly on my chest," he said, and he slid his hands down her back to her hips, "and your hips feel just right against mine."

She swiveled her hips against his. "Yes, they do. Are you sure you don't want to stay with me tonight?"

"No, I'm not sure," he said, but he wasn't going to. He wanted Selena but he wanted her on his terms. And that meant having her respect. She was going to be a vacation fling, not a one-night stand. So he slowly drew her arms down from his shoulders and gave her a kiss that almost killed him when he pulled away.

"Good night, Selena," he said and then walked out of her suite and went down the hall to his.

Vacation affair be damned, he already cared about her more than he wanted to admit.

Seven

Two days later, Selena wasn't too sure how she found herself on Justin's yacht sailing around Biscayne Bay.

True, he hadn't given up his pursuit of her at all. She'd been surprised when he'd taken a suite on the same floor as her at the Ritz but she shouldn't have been. He was a very thorough man.

"I forgot how much I like Miami," she said.

"And the nights here?" he asked. She stood next to him in the cockpit while he piloted the boat. He'd told her when they arrived that he had a staff of three, but most of the time preferred to do short trips by himself.

"Definitely. I love the nights," she said, putting her hand on his shoulder and rubbing it. She liked the way his hard muscles felt under the cloth of his dress shirt.

"I thought the committee meeting went well today," he said.

She shook her head. "We're on vacation, so we can't talk business."

He arched one eyebrow at her. "Are you sure?"

She nodded. She'd had fevered dreams of Justin for the last two nights. Since she'd met him he was someone she just couldn't turn her back on, and tonight with the sea breeze in her hair and the smell of the ocean surrounding her, she realized she wasn't going to just walk away from Justin Stern. It might not be the smartest thing she ever did but she knew she was going to have an affair with this man.

She wanted to know the man beneath the clothes. The one that few others had seen and that would belong to only her.

Belong to her? she wondered. Did she really want him to be hers? She wanted him in her bed taking care of her sexual needs, but for anything else?

"Very sure. But it's a fling, Justin, it can't be more than that."

"I agree. Do you mind helping me out with dinner?"

"Uh, I guess not. I should tell you my culinary skills are limited," she said. "I live on takeout and microwave dinners."

"They must agree with you," he said, skimming his gaze over her body, lingering at her curves.

"They do. What do you need from me?" she asked.

"I have a picnic basket on the table in the galley and a bottle of pinot grigio chilling in the wine refrigerator. Will you bring them up?"

"Yes, are we dining on the deck?"

"Yes, aft…you'll see where the cushions are set up. I'm going to find a safe place to drop anchor and then I'll meet you down there," he said.

She moved to go past him down the short flight of stairs but he stopped her with a hand on her waist.

"Yes?"

"I'm very glad we have this time together," he said. It was one of those awkward things that he sometimes said that made her heart skip a beat. He was sweet when he wasn't so arrogant and cocky.

"Me, too," she said.

He leaned down and rubbed his lips over hers. His breath was minty but when he opened his mouth and his tongue swept into hers she tasted *him*. She held on to his shoulders; he deepened the kiss and she realized this was what she'd been craving. This was what she needed.

She'd been alone too long. Working to forget the pain she'd run from and afraid to take a chance on being with another man. Now Justin seemed like he was the remedy.

They hit a wave and it jarred them off balance. She fell into Justin, who was careful to keep them both on their feet.

"I better pay attention to where we are going," he said.

"Yes, you better. I have plans for you," she said.

He wriggled his eyebrows at her. "You do?"

"Indeed…you mentioned a bottle of wine and I might need a big strong man to open it for me."

He threw his head back and laughed. She smiled at him. This was what she needed. A nice break from a long day of negotiating. And it didn't matter that she was with the man who'd been arguing with her all day.

She climbed down the steps and went into the galley. She'd been on yachts before and though there was luxury in every inch of the boat it didn't make her feel uncomfortable. Justin had made this place homey. Selena's favorite touch was a picture on the galley wall of Justin and his brothers, all shirtless and looking yummy, playing a beach volleyball game.

She leaned in closer for a better look at the photo and realized that Justin had a scar on his sternum. Reaching out she traced the line and wondered how he got it. There was so much more to him than what she knew from the boardroom, but she knew she had to be cautious with him on their personal time.

If this was going to be a fling, then she shouldn't know too much about him. How was that going to work? She wanted to know everything about Justin. She needed to figure out what made him tick so she could make sure he didn't get the upper hand on her.

Could she do it?

Hell, she knew she was going to try. She wasn't about to walk away from him whether that was wise or not.

She heard the engine stop and the whir as he dropped anchor and realized she was staring at his photo instead of doing what he'd asked of her.

She opened the wine refrigerator and grabbed a bottle of Coppola Pinot Grigio and then picked up the picnic basket, which was heavy.

She emerged from the galley just as he came down from the pilot deck.

"Let me get the basket," he said.

She handed it over to him and followed him to the back of the boat where he'd already arranged some cushions. With a flick of a button, music started playing. She shivered a little as she realized that this evening was part of a fantasy she'd always harbored. Not one she'd ever told another soul about but somehow Justin had gleaned enough from her to know that this was what she'd always wanted.

Justin had always loved the water. It was the one place where he and his brothers had been alone with their father. Since his mother got seasick she never came out on the boat with them.

His dad had taught all three of the boys everything they needed to know about sailing—and navigating the waters around *her*. But that was it. He didn't have any useful lessons when it came to women. As Justin and his brothers had gotten older, their father merely warned them not to fall in love.

Love is a sweet trap, my boys, Justin remembered his father saying.

Sitting on the deck in the moonlight, listening to the soft voice of Selena, Justin couldn't see what his father had meant. Not with this woman.

"Dinner was very nice," she said. "Though I don't know that your culinary skills are any better than mine."

"Just because I had a little help from Publix?" he asked.

"Yes. And I am going to treat you to dinner tomorrow night."

"You are?" he asked. Perfect, he already planned for the two of them to spend every night together. It would be difficult later in the month as he started to have commitments with the tenth anniversary celebration. He knew he needed to make every minute with her count.

"Definitely. I will even cook for you. The one dish I know how to make."

"What is it?" he asked, suspecting that she must be

able to cook even though she said she mostly had others cooking for her. He did the same thing because when you only cooked for one it wasn't that much fun.

"A traditional Cuban one. I'm not going to say any more. I want you to be surprised."

"I already am. I thought you were never going to ask me out," he said with a mock frown.

"I haven't had a chance. You've been hitting on me since we met. I couldn't get a word in edgewise."

"It's your fault."

"How do you figure?" she asked.

"You are one hot mama! I knew I couldn't let the chance to get to know you pass me by."

She put her wineglass down and moved over so she was sitting next to him. She had her legs curved under her body and as she leaned forward her blouse shifted, and he glimpsed the curve of her breasts encased in a pretty pink bra.

"I am so glad you didn't," she said in a soft, seductive voice.

Everything masculine in him went on point and he knew that he was tired of waiting. Tired of playing it safe with her. Life seldom offered him a chance like Selena represented. She was everything he wanted in a woman.

He reached out and touched her, tracing the line of her shirt and the soft skin underneath. She shifted her shoulders as she reached for him.

"Unbutton your shirt," she said. "I want to see your chest."

"You do?" he asked.

She nibbled on her lower lip as she nodded at him.

"You do it," he said.

She arched one eyebrow at him. "I should have guessed you'd want to be in charge here."

"I am always in charge," he said, bringing her hands to his mouth and placing a wet, hot kiss in the center of her palms before putting her hands on his chest.

She took her time toying with the buttons, caressing his chest as she undid each one. She paused at the scar on his sternum; she traced the edges of it with her forefinger.

"How did you get this?"

"I wish I had some glamorous tale to tell you but it happened when I was in college—young and a little bit reckless, I'm afraid."

"How?"

"It's not sexy, let's not talk about it," he said.

"I want to know. I have a long scar on my thigh which I might show you if you tell me how you got this," she said, running the edge of her nail over the line of the scar.

He shuddered in reaction, loving her hands on his body. He was intrigued, too, wanted to see her thighs and what she was talking about.

He took her hand in his and rubbed it on his chest where she'd been stroking him. "Frat party plus pretty girls plus impulsive need to show off equaled this scar."

She started laughing. "I wouldn't have pegged you for the show-off type."

"I guess I'm not trying hard enough if you can't see me strutting my stuff to get your attention."

She leaned in close, coming up on her knees and putting both hands on his shoulders. "You have my attention, Mr. Stern. What are you going to do with it?"

He put his hands on her waist and drew her even

closer to him until she was straddling his hips and her skirt fell over his lap. When she shifted, he felt the core of her body brush over his erection.

"I guess I have your attention," she said.

"You do. Now about that scar on your thigh," he said.

"I haven't decided if you've told me enough to get to see it."

"I am going to see it," he said, sliding his hands up under her skirt and caressing every inch of her thigh. He couldn't feel anything on her left thigh but on her right one there was a slight abrasion. "I think I've found it."

"You have," she confirmed. Then she leaned down to kiss him and he let her take control of this moment.

Justin's hands slid up and down her back and she forgot everything but the sensations he evoked in her. She put her mind on hold and just reveled in the sensation of being on the sea on this beautiful warm night with this man who wanted nothing but her body.

There was a freedom in this that she had never experienced before. A freedom to be here with him. It didn't matter that later she might regret this. Right now it was exactly what she needed.

"Why did you stop kissing me?" he asked.

"I'm trying not to think," she said. "It's not working."

"Then I'm not doing my job," he said. "I should be sweeping you away from your worries."

"You should be…I think talking isn't going to help. Why don't you put your mouth on me and make me forget."

He arched one eyebrow at her. "Do I have that power over you?"

"You have no idea," she admitted.

She had tried to justify this attraction, to blame it on the fact that she was back in Miami. But that wasn't it—she knew it was Justin, pure and simple.

She wanted his mouth on hers. She needed his hands sliding over her body, and she had to touch him. She was tired of being good and living an honest life. Not that there was anything dishonest about this, but she just needed a chance to let loose and Justin had offered her that.

"Kiss me."

"Yes," he said. His mouth found hers. He sucked her lower lip between his teeth and held it gently there while he suckled.

She swept her hands under his shirt enjoying the warmth of his skin and the strength of his muscles under her fingers. She liked the light dusting of hair on his chest and how it felt as she ran her hands over him. She lingered at his scar, tracing the outside edges of it and then followed the trail of hair as it narrowed on his chest and dipped into his waistband.

She pulled back so she could see him. He lounged back against the pillows and cushions with his shirt open. He looked like a pasha of old and she felt like a willing sex slave sent to please him.

She shifted back so her thighs rested on her heels. She pushed his shirt off his shoulders and he pulled his arms out of it.

He reached for the sash on the left side of her blouse and undid it. As the fabric fell open he put his hands on her waist and drew her up and back over his thighs. He reached under her shirt, his large hands rubbing over her bare midriff and then spanning her waist.

"You are so tiny," he said.

"I'm not," she said. She was an average-size girl; it was just that Justin was a big man with big hands.

He pushed her blouse off her shoulders and it fell off her arms behind her. He brought his hand up and slowly traced the pattern of her bra. Traced it from her clavicle down her chest to the curve of her breast.

He ran his finger down the edge where the cup met the other and then back up. She had goose bumps on her chest and her nipples stirred inside the cups of her bra. Wanting to feel that firm finger of his on them.

He reached behind her and undid the clasp and then carefully peeled the cups away until her breasts were revealed to him. He dropped the bra on the deck where her blouse was.

He cupped both breasts in his hands, letting his big palms rub both of her nipples in a circular motion. The sensation started a chain reaction in her. She loved the feeling and shifted her hips against his erection to satisfy the ache that started at the apex of her thighs.

He spread his fingers out, caressing the full globes of her breasts, and then slowly drew his right hand up to the tip of her nipple. But he didn't linger there.

He circled her areola with his forefinger and then bent forward, holding her back with one hand. She felt the brush of his breath against her nipple as it tightened and then a tiny lick of his tongue.

"More," she said. She was desperate to feel his entire mouth on her nipple. "Suckle me."

He shook his head and she felt his silky hair against her breast as he continued to trace over her breast and nipple with his tongue.

The crotch of her panties was moist and she felt almost desperate to feel more of his mouth against her.

She tried to shift her shoulders and force him to take more of her nipple but he just pulled his head back.

"Not until I'm ready," he said.

"Be ready," she ordered him.

He gave her a purely sexual smile. "Not yet."

He treated her other breast to the same delicate teasing and she was squirming on his lap when he lifted his head. But when she put her hands on his chest and saw him shiver, she knew she had her own power over him.

And it was intoxicating. Leaning forward she tunneled her fingers through his hair and let the tips of her breasts brush against this chest.

He moaned, the sound low and husky.

"Do you like that?" she asked, whispering into his ear.

"Very much," he said. Using his grip on her waist he pushed her back into the cushions and came over her.

His hips were cradled between her thighs and his arms braced his weight above her. He rotated his hips and his erection pressed against the very center of her.

She moaned softly and he leaned down over her.

"Do you like that?"

"Yesss."

He smiled down at her and lowered his head to her body. He used his mouth at her neck and nibbled his way down to her breasts.

He cupped them in his hands as she undulated under him, trying to get closer to what she needed. And what she needed was this man. She needed to feel him naked above her and hot and hard inside her.

She shifted her legs, curving her thigh up around his hips. The position shifted him against her and he said her name in a low, feral tone of voice.

He didn't stop in his slow seduction but his hands swept down her body and she felt her skirt slowly lifted until the juncture of their bodies wouldn't allow it to come any farther up. She lifted her hips and moaned as the tip of his shaft rubbed her.

He pushed her skirt higher and then she felt his hands on her butt. He rubbed his palm over her and then pulled her skimpy bikini panties down. He leaned up over her, kneeling between her legs as he stripped them off.

He tossed them aside and looked down at her. His chest rose and fell with each breath he took and his skin was flushed.

His erection was visible behind the zipper of his pants and she felt another surge of power that she affected him so visibly.

She lifted her arms behind her head and twined her fingers together, the movement forcing her breasts forward.

He watched each move she made. She brought her left leg up and then slowly let it fall wide, exposing her very center to him. He put his hand on her ankles and drew her legs open even farther and then leaned forward.

"You are truly the most beautiful woman I've ever seen," he said. "I want to take my time and explore every inch of you, but my body wants something else."

"What do you want, Justin?"

"To hear you moaning my name while I'm buried inside of your silky hot body."

"Me, too," she said. This wasn't about power but about pleasure. And it had been too long since she'd enjoyed a man just for the pure thrill of it.

"Come to me," she said.

He shook his head. "No. I want to make this last. I

want to make you come so much that you forget every other man but me."

She tipped her head to the side studying him. He'd already wiped every man from her mind. She only saw him. She'd dreamed of him before this…was this a mistake?

She shook her head as she felt his hands on her again. She didn't care if this wasn't smart. She wanted Justin and she was going to have him. Tomorrow she'd sort out the problems this brought to her. This night was hers.

She felt the warmth of his breath on her stomach and his finger caressing the outer edge of her belly button. He drew his hands down her hips, then down farther until he found that scar on her thigh. He traced it with his finger, then lightly with his tongue.

His mouth on her sent pulses of warmth through her core and she knew she was close to orgasm. Every pleasure point she had was pulsing.

He parted her thighs and dropped nibbling kisses up their length. His fingers skimmed over her feminine secrets and then came back. He rubbed his palm over her center and her hips jerked upward.

She felt the cool night air on her most private flesh before his breath bathed her. His tongue danced over her flesh and she clenched her thighs around his head. He put one of his hands on her stomach and shifted between her legs, lying down there.

He lifted his head and looked up the length of her body. Their eyes met and something passed between them. She didn't know what but she felt like he'd found a secret she'd kept hidden even from herself.

He lowered his head again and when he sucked on her intimate flesh everything inside of her clenched. Her breasts felt too full, her nipples were tight little points and she was wet and dripping. She wanted him inside of her and she grabbed at his shoulders hoping to hurry him. To make him come up over her. But he stayed where he was.

His tongue and teeth were driving her toward a climax, which felt too intense. She lifted her thighs and held his head to her body with her hands in his thick silky hair. She arched her hips as she came in a blinding rush.

"Justin, yes, keep doing that," she cried out. She couldn't stop the sensations rushing through her. They were intense and almost scary in the pleasure they created.

He kept his mouth on her until she stopped trembling in his arms. She tugged at his shoulders, wanting him to come up over her. But he sat back on his heels between her legs and watched her.

She wanted to give him the same pleasure he'd given her. She sat up and pushed him back against the pillows and reached for his zipper, carefully lowering it and freeing his erection from his boxers. There was a tip of moisture at the tip and he shuddered when she wiped it off with her finger and brought it to her mouth to lick it.

He tasted salty and vaguely like his kisses. She stroked his shaft from the root to the tip, swiping her finger over the tip each time. With her other hand she cupped him and squeezed gently.

His breath sawed from his body as he grew even harder in her hand. She leaned forward and let her hair brush over his erection. He shuddered again and his hands burrowed into her hair as his hips came forward and the tip of his erection touched her lips.

She licked the tip and then took him into her mouth.

He moaned that deep guttural sound of his again. She loved the feeling of him in her mouth. He was too big for her to take his entire length but she stroked her hand on him and drew her mouth up and over him, sweeping her tongue over the tip.

His hands tightened in her hair and he drew her off his body. "No more. I need to be inside you."

"Now?" she asked. It was what she was craving, too.

"Now," he said, pushing her onto her back and coming down between her legs. He found her opening with the tip of his erection and it was the naked flesh-on-flesh moment that jarred her.

"You feel so good," he said. "Should I get a condom?"

"I'm on the Pill," she said.

"Good," he said and thrust into her.

She came in that instant, just a tiny fluttering of a climax as he filled her all the way to her womb. His abdomen hit her in the right spot and he drew back and entered her again. Slow, long thrusts that made her moan and writhe beneath him.

His chest and shoulders were above her and she held him tight, lifted herself closer to him. "You feel so good."

"So do you," he said. His hips moved with surety between her legs until she was overwhelmed with the feel of him.

The hair on his chest abraded her aroused nipples and she shuddered again as she felt everything inside of her building to another climax. And this one felt even more intense than the other two he'd given her.

He put his hands under her, cupping her buttocks in his hands and lifting her hips higher so that he could get

Get 2 Books FREE!

Silhouette® Books,
publisher of women's fiction,
presents

EE BOOKS!   Use the reply card inside to get two free books!

EE GIFTS!   You'll also get two exciting surprise gifts, absolutely free!

GET 2 BOOKS

We'd like to send you two *Silhouette Desire®* novels absolutely free.
Accepting them puts you under no obligation to purchase any more books

HOW TO GET YOUR
2 FREE BOOKS AND 2 FREE GIFTS

1. Return the reply card today, and we'll send you two *Silhouette Desire* novels, absolutely free! We'll even pay the postage!

2. Accepting free books places you under no obligation to buy anything, ever. Whatever you decide, the free books and gifts are yours to keep, free!

3. We hope that after receiving your free books you'll want to remain a subscriber, but the choice is yours—to continue or cancel, any time at all!

EXTRA BONUS

You'll also get two free mystery gifts! (worth about $10)

FREE!

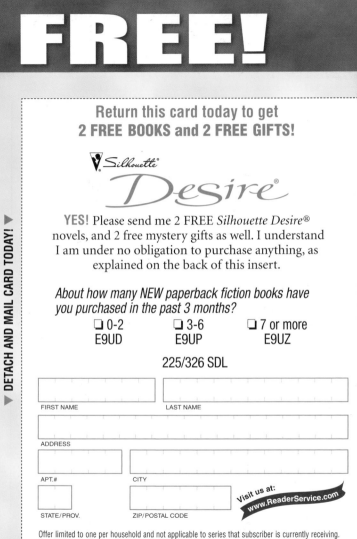

Return this card today to get
2 FREE BOOKS and 2 FREE GIFTS!

Silhouette Desire®

YES! Please send me 2 FREE *Silhouette Desire®* novels, and 2 free mystery gifts as well. I understand I am under no obligation to purchase anything, as explained on the back of this insert.

About how many NEW paperback fiction books have you purchased in the past 3 months?

❑ 0-2
E9UD

❑ 3-6
E9UP

❑ 7 or more
E9UZ

225/326 SDL

FIRST NAME

LAST NAME

ADDRESS

APT.#

CITY

STATE/PROV.

ZIP/POSTAL CODE

Visit us at:
www.ReaderService.com

▲ DETACH AND MAIL CARD TODAY! ▲

(S-D-03/11)

deeper on each thrust. He leaned over her, whispering dark sex words into her ear and she felt the first fingers of her orgasm teasing her. Making her shiver under him. Then he drew back and thrust heavily into her, his hips moving faster and faster until she screamed with her climax.

She felt his hips continue to jerk forward and the warmth of his seed spilling inside of her. He thrust two more times before collapsing on her. He breathed heavily and his body was bathed in sweat. She wrapped her arms and legs around him and held him to her like she'd never have to let go.

She looked up at the night sky and realized that she really didn't want to have to let him go.

Eight

The last thing that Justin wanted to do was get up and move away from Selena. Holding her in his arms was the most addicting thing he'd ever done. But the sea breezes were getting stronger and he knew they couldn't stay on the deck all night. He slipped out of her and rolled to his side, coming up on his elbow.

Her lips were swollen from his kisses and her eyes sleepy as she looked up at him. He drew one finger over her lips and then realized that he was never going to get enough of her. He was spent from making love but he still wanted to lie next to her and hold her in his arms.

That was dangerous stuff.

Tomas Gonzalez may have found the one weakness that Justin had. One he himself hadn't realized until this very second.

"I guess we have to get up," she said.

"I was thinking about carrying you down to the bedroom."

"What are you waiting for?"

He scooped her up in his arms and then stood up. He liked the feel of her there. She wrapped one arm around his shoulders and her long, silky hair rubbed against his arm as he carried her down the stairs.

The stairs were narrow but he turned to enable them both to fit. She felt right here—in his arms and on his yacht.

He glanced down, noticing she stared up at him. "What are you thinking?"

"That this was exactly what I needed," she said.

He felt the same way but he'd never admit that out loud. Already he knew that if he was going to continue to keep control over this affair he needed to play his cards close to his chest. Make love to her—he knew he had to keep doing that. There was no way this one time had satiated him. He was satisfied but he still craved more.

He laid her on the center of his bed with the navy blue comforter and stood next to her. He wanted this to be more than he knew it could be. More than she wanted from him. But it wasn't.

"I have to wash up," he said. It wasn't romantic but then sex technically wasn't supposed to be about romance. It was dirty, hot and sweaty and it made him feel very primitive and possessive. Especially with her.

He padded in his bare feet to the head and washed up quickly, bringing a warm washcloth back to the bed to gently wash between her legs. She was still where he'd left her and when he pulled the covers back and laid down, she curled onto her side and put her arm around his waist.

He put his arm around her and drew her closer to him. The soft exhalation of her breath stirred the hair on his chest. And it was only as the moonlight trickled through the porthole window that he realized she hadn't said anything since he'd carried her downstairs.

"Are you okay?" he asked, rubbing his arm up and down hers.

She shrugged.

"Selena?"

"Yes?"

"Talk to me," he said. He wanted to know her secrets and this moment was as close as they were going to get to really seeing the truth in each other. They were both vulnerable.

Yes, he realized, she was vulnerable. That wasn't what he intended to make her feel but he was very glad that what they'd shared had affected her.

"I'm not sure what to say. I thought that I'd have an affair with you and still be able to keep you off your toes in the boardroom but now I'm second-guessing that. I'm not sure that this was wise," she said.

He tipped her head up to him so that their eyes met. "I'm not sure it was, either, but I don't think we could have waited much longer for this."

"Why?"

He needed her but he wasn't going to admit it. "The attraction between us is very strong."

"Yes, it is."

"I for one was distracted all day today by the small glimpses I got of your cleavage each time you leaned forward to gesture to something on the map."

She laughed, and it was a sweet sound. "I will have to remember that."

"I have no doubt that you will. Let's not overthink this," he said. "We are two people out of time here. Our ordinary worlds are far away and for now there is only the two of us."

"You make it sound so simple and so appealing. But I know that every action has a reaction."

"And every reaction is bad?" he asked.

"Not at all. But every reaction causes ripples and I don't want to hurt my grandparents...not again."

He shifted them on the bed so she was lying on her back and he was next to her propped up on his elbow.

"Tell me about it," he invited. "Whatever it is that you did to hurt them before."

She brought her arms up to her waist and hugged herself and he didn't like that. He was here with her now; she should turn to him for comfort.

He stroked her arm and she patted his hand.

"I don't think it's the right story for tonight but I will tell you about it sometime."

"Tomorrow?" he asked. "After you cook me dinner."

"Stop being so bossy," she said, but she smiled when she said that, so he suspected she didn't really mind.

"It's part of my charm."

"You always put such a heavy burden on your charm."

"And it doesn't measure up?"

"You measure up just fine," she said, sweeping her hands down his chest and cupping him in her hand.

He was no longer interested in talking and instead made love to her in his bed, then held her quietly in his arms afterward as they both drifted to sleep.

* * *

The next morning, Justin showered in the guest room while Selena used the master bathroom. He gathered her clothing first and left it lying on the bed so she'd find it when she came out.

He hadn't planned on making love to her last night, but then he hadn't planned on much when it came to Selena Gonzalez.

She totally knocked him for a loop. Since the first time he'd laid eyes on her he'd been lost. That wasn't right, he was a very successful businessman and he didn't get lost. He always had a motivation for everything he did. He had to remember that Selena wasn't only an attractive woman, she was also a powerful adversary.

That's right, he was doing what he had to in order to ensure that Luna Azul continued to prosper. And no matter that he was determined to keep the personal and business parts of their lives separate, he knew something had changed between them last night.

His BlackBerry pinged and he glanced at the screen to see the reminder of his 10:00 a.m. tee time with Maxwell Strong. He still had an hour but getting the boat back to the marina and then dropping Selena at the Ritz was going to eat into his time.

He got dressed and checked the master bedroom. Selena's clothes were gone. When he got upstairs, he found her sitting on the bench at the stern of the boat. She had on a pair of huge sunglasses that covered not only her eyes but also most of her face.

She might be wearing yesterday's clothing but she didn't seem unkempt. In fact she looked cool and remote—untouchable.

He paused and studied her, realizing that just because he'd had her body last night didn't mean he'd come close to unraveling all the secrets that made Selena who she was.

"Ready to head back to the real world?" he asked.

She tipped her head to the side and studied him. "I guess we have to. I have a meeting this morning that I'm going to be late for unless we get moving."

"I have one as well," he said. "I have a Keurig machine in the galley if you want some coffee."

"No thanks. I'm a tea drinker," she said.

"I wouldn't have pegged you for one," he said, climbing the stairs to the pilot house.

He glanced over his shoulder and saw that she'd followed him.

"Why not?"

"You just don't look the type."

"There's a tea type?" she asked.

A part of him knew it was time to let this conversation drop but another part was just dying to see how she'd react. "Yes, I'm thinking white-haired old ladies sitting around in homemade sweaters, having little cakes and drinking tea out of pots covered in quilted cozies."

She punched him in the arm. "Not only old ladies drink tea. And those cozies can be very nicely made."

"I told you I didn't see you as a tea drinker."

"You aren't winning any points for that," she said.

He pushed the button to turn on the engines and the boat roared to life. But he didn't really want to head back to the port. He wanted to stay out here on the sea with just Selena. If he were a different man he'd ask her to run away with him or maybe just kidnap her and sail off for some exotic port of call, but he wasn't.

And they both had family to think of. The Gonzalez family would probably crucify him if he tried to abduct their prodigal daughter.

"Why are you looking at me like that?"

"I'm contemplating kidnapping you and keeping you naked in my bed."

She shook her head. "You'd never do it. You'd never let your brothers down like that."

"You wouldn't go for it either. I bet you'd jump over-board and swim back to Miami if I tried it."

She shrugged. "Maybe."

He steered them to the harbor, the engines and the sea wind whipping around them. "No maybe about it. You feel guilty where your grandparents are concerned and you'll do whatever you have to in order to make them proud this time."

She wrapped an arm around her waist and turned away from him, staring out over the horizon. He wondered if she'd really be happy running away with him. Lord knew he was tempted, but she had been right. He would never do that until he had everything settled for Luna Azul. It wasn't just a company he worked for, it was his family legacy, and he wasn't about to lose it.

"When are you going to trust me with your past?" he asked her.

"Tonight," she said. "I want you to come to my house. It will be easier to talk about the past if you are there. But if we do this…we won't be a vacation fling anymore."

"Are you sure you want to chance it?"

She studied him for a long minute and he had the feeling that she was searching for answers in his face. He wanted her to find what she was looking for but this morning he didn't have any notion of what she needed from him. After making love to her last night he'd thought he'd know her better but instead he found she was still a mystery to him.

"Yes. I think that we have to keep moving forward. I don't want to walk away…not yet."

He knew that the end was possible—even probable given the way they'd come together—and he was bracing himself for it. Still, starting a relationship and expecting it to end wasn't the best idea.

"We're like a short-term partnership," he said.

"Trust you to put it in terms that would be better suited to the boardroom, but yes, that's exactly what we are. It will be mutually advantageous to both of us while it lasts."

"And pleasurable," he added. He slowed the boat as they reached the marina and he maneuvered his yacht into its slip before turning off the engine.

"What time tonight?" he asked her.

"Seven? Is that too early?"

He took her hand and led her down the gangway to the deck. "No, it sounds just right. Do you want me to drop you at the Ritz?"

"Yes, please," she said.

He drove her to the hotel and let her off, then watched her walk away. He pulled back out into traffic before she was inside the hotel because he didn't want to sit there and think about how hard it was to let her go.

Nine

Selena drove through Miami like the devil himself was chasing her. She wanted to escape her thoughts. It wasn't that she was afraid of Justin; it was simply that he represented a part of her that she wanted to pretend didn't exist anymore. She wanted to drive away from the area and never look back. But running away wasn't her style any more, either.

She pulled into the parking lot of Luna Azul. At a little after ten on Tuesday morning there wasn't much action here. She had an appointment with Justin's older brother, Cam. Through the grapevine she'd heard that he had been the one to raise his younger brothers after both parents were killed. Cam had been twenty at the time.

She pushed her sunglasses up on her head as she entered the cool dark interior of Luna Azul. The club was gorgeous with a huge Chihuly installation in the foyer. The building had once been a cigar factory back in the early 1900s. It was inspired by the success of Ybor Haya's factories in Key West and Ybor City near Tampa Bay.

The Miami factory had been started by the Jimenez brothers and prospered for several years until cigarettes became more popular and eventually the company went out of business. When Selena had been growing up this factory was a derelict building that was a breeding ground for gang-related trouble.

Seeing it today, she had to admit that the Stern brothers had improved this corner of their neighborhood.

"You must be Selena."

She glanced up as Cam Stern walked toward her. He was the same height as Justin and they both had the same stubborn-looking jaw, but there the resemblance ended. Justin was simply a better-looking man. Where Justin's eyes were blue, Cam's were dark obsidian, and Cam wore his hair long enough to brush his shoulders.

"I am indeed. You must be Cam," she said, holding out her hand.

He shook her hand firmly and then let it drop. "I'm glad you could come down here. I wanted you to see what we've been doing here in the last ten years and why it's important that we get the Mercado project going so we can revitalize the area the way we did with the club."

"No one doubts you can pour money into a project and make it successful. I've said as much to Justin. The Gonzalez family is concerned that you are going to take away a vital community shopping center and make it an upscale shopping area of no use to the local residents. We aren't interested in having more of the celebrities you bring down here socializing while families are trying to buy their groceries."

Cam tilted his head to the side. "I can see that you have inherited your grandfather's fire."

"I'm flattered you think so, but I'm not half as obstinate as he is."

Cam laughed as she'd hoped he would. And she realized that Cam was a nice guy. Not because of the laughter but because he'd asked for this meeting. She suspected that he was trying to help her and the rest of the committee understand and see the human face of Luna Azul.

"I grew up here on Fisher Island, Selena—is it okay to call you by your first name?" he asked.

"Of course, I'm planning to call you Cam."

He smiled at her. "Let's go up to the rooftop. I want to show you our club up there."

"I want to see it. My younger brother has told me that he is interested in deejaying here and he has heard that the rooftop club is all Latin music."

"That's right. We start each evening with a couple of professional dancers teaching our guests how to salsa. Then we have a conga line to get them out there onto the dance floor."

"Sounds fun. One thing that Enrique also mentioned is that most of the staff isn't from our neighborhood."

"That's true. We had so much resistance from the local leaders when we bought the club that I didn't get any local talent auditioning for the roles we had. I had to look beyond Little Havana to find the people I needed," he said. "But that's beginning to change."

For the first time she truly understood how hard it must have been for the Sterns to come in here and try to open this place up. And when they got off the elevator at the rooftop club she was astounded by the feel and look of it. To be honest she felt like she was stepping into one of her grandfather's pictures of old Havana.

"This is perfect," she said. "My *abuelito* would love this. It looks like the patio where he and my grandmother met."

"Thank you," Cam said. "We spent a lot of time trying to capture the feeling of Cuba pre-Castro."

"You did it. But why did you choose to build here? You could have chosen downtown Miami or South Beach and not encountered any resistance."

He glanced out in the distance where the skyline of Miami was visible. "I wanted to be a part of this community. When I was a boy we had a nanny from Little Havana and Maria used to tell me stories of Cuba when she'd put us to bed each night."

"That's sweet. So you did it for her?"

He arched one eyebrow at her in a way that reminded her of his brother. Justin was in her mind today. No matter what she tried, he wasn't going to be easy to relegate out of her head.

"I did it because this building came on the market—it had been foreclosed on. It was a bargain. Justin was still in college and it was before Nate made it big in baseball. I had Maria's stories and a building I could afford and I thought I might have a chance at making this work—about as much a chance as a blue moon."

"A slim one," she said.

He nodded and despite the fact that he was supposed to be the big bad corporate enemy of her grandparents she understood that he and his family had come to this neighborhood the same way her family had. Looking for a chance to put down roots and make their fortune.

* * *

The Florida sun was bright and hot as Justin drove his golf cart over the course. Next to him Maxwell talked about his daughter's impending high school graduation and the fact that she was making him nuts.

"I thought kids were easier once they were no longer toddlers," Justin said.

"That's a lie parents try to spread around to convince other adults to join their club of misery," Maxwell said with a laugh.

"I know you'd do it again," Justin said.

"I would. She's a great kid. It's just since January she's been like a crazy person. Her moods swing and she goes from being so mature I can see the woman she's become to being more irrational that she was when she was six. It's crazy. But I know you don't want to hear about that."

"Nah, I don't mind hearing about your family. You give me a little insight into how the other half lives."

"Ever think of joining the married ranks?" Maxwell asked.

"Haven't found the right girl yet," Justin said, but that was his standard line. The truth was that he was married to his work. But he wouldn't mind making a little more time for Selena. That thought slipped through without him realizing it.

He wondered what their children would look like— what?! Hell, no he didn't wonder about that. He was focused on the Mercado and making that successful. "It'd be hard to have a wife when I have to spend all my hours at the office trying to figure out things like this zoning hiccup."

Maxwell laughed. "I knew that was the real reason you invited me out here today."

"Hey, I listened to your kid's stories," Justin said with a grin. He and Maxwell were friends; they'd played together on the same beach volleyball team a few summers ago.

Maxwell had also been very helpful when Cam had wanted to add the rooftop club to Luna Azul. There had been an issue with the noise and it had taken some careful negotiating with Maxwell and the zoning office to get that taken care of.

"That you did. Well near as I can tell you aren't in any direct violation of zoning laws with your proposed marketplace. There is an ordinance in that area that specifies we have to bid the work out to local craftsmen before giving you the go ahead. So if you told me you were getting bids from all Little Havana companies I'd see no reason to deny you the building permits you need."

Justin nodded. That made sense. He pulled to a stop at the seventh hole and Maxwell got out and set up his shot. He had the committee to think about and knowing them as he was coming to, he thought he could get them to recommend the construction companies he used for bids.

"What about the vendors?"

"You have to use a local vendor to replace an existing local vendor. So in your plaza, you have a Cuban American grocery store. If you want to get rid of the one there you have to go with a local chain. You might be able to get a Publix in there but nothing national. I think I saw Whole Foods on your specs, that won't be possible."

Justin wasn't surprised. "Is that legal?"

"Pretty much. You can file a lawsuit if you want but it will take you years to get it through the court system.

It's easier to just work with the local business owners and get them on your team."

"That's what you think," Justin said.

Maxwell laughed. "Your problem is that you are used to being the boss. You might have to compromise."

"No way," Justin said with a pretend frown. "Seriously, I have a committee that has local business owners on it so I think we should be able to get some movement on this soon. What do you need from me?"

"Some quiet so I can take my stroke," Maxwell said.

Justin was quiet as Maxwell took his shot and got close to the hole. Justin had played this course a million times since he was a boy. His father had taught him to play here at the country club and he was normally able to make a hole-in-one on this green.

He lined up and took his shot landing it in the hole. Maxwell whistled but they had played together before and pretending he couldn't do something when he could went against Justin's grain.

"I need to see three bids from the construction companies you are using, making sure at least one is local to Little Havana and then you are good to go. Don't forget what I said about the tenants because they won't."

"I hear that. You know when Cam first bought the club they wanted nothing to do with him so we never considered that they'd want to be part of the marketplace," Justin said.

"You are in a different place than you were then. I'm just guessing here but seeing the success you guys have made of Luna Azul probably has a lot of business owners at that strip mall hoping that you can do the same thing to their businesses, which is why they don't want you to use outside vendors this time."

"It's nice to see how much ten years has changed things," Justin said.

"It is. Sitting in my office it's hard to remember ten years ago, I mean I'm looking at changes in some areas that we thought we'd never see. Swampy area that is now being zoned commercial. That's crazy, man."

"It is," Justin said. The conversation turned to the Miami Heat's chances of making the finals this year and they finished their round of golf. Justin knew that he'd learned nothing that he couldn't have found out from talking to Maxwell on the phone but this had been nicer and for a few hours he'd been able to stop thinking of Selena and how she'd felt in his arms last night.

The committee meeting was scheduled for five o'clock that evening and Selena arrived ten minutes late because her grandmother had found out she wasn't staying in her house and had wanted to talk. Luckily Selena's brother had stepped in and gotten their grandmother off her back so that she didn't have to delve into why she owned a home and didn't want to stay there.

Selena thought a woman as superstitious as her *abuelita* would just understand about ghosts from the past and memories that lingered in a place.

She also thought her reasons would be obvious to anyone who'd known what she'd been through with Raul. She thought a bit more about how she'd let him steal so much from her. Not just her grandparents' money but also the home she'd inherited from her great aunt. It wasn't full of childhood memories but it had been a place that Selena had made into a home and Raul had stolen the safety of that home from her.

Tonight she realized was her chance to return and maybe reclaim it. It wasn't lost on her that she was inviting a man she wasn't sure she could trust to help her do that.

She walked into the downtown offices of the Luna Azul Company fully expecting to see Justin in the conference room but instead Cam was there. She frowned but then told herself that didn't matter. This was the business side of their relationship.

Did they have a personal side? She felt like they were lovers and that was it. She had to remember there was no relationship. It didn't matter that she had slept in his arms, there wasn't anything permanent between them.

The room was filled with her friends and cousins. The community leaders were her family. Everyone with a stake in the Mercado was here.

"Justin is running late today. And now that Selena is here we can get started. I'm happy to say that after meeting with Selena and talking to Justin, I think we can come up with a solution that will work for all of us."

"We will see," her grandfather said.

"I think you'll be pleased, Tomas," Cam said. "I feel like I should apologize for not coming to the community leaders before you went to the zoning commission. It is just that ten years ago when we opened the club no one wanted us to be a part of the community."

"Times have changed," Selena said. "Now what is it you have to offer us?"

"First off we would like to hire a local construction company to do the renovations and Justin is going to bring the solicitation for bids. Can you recommend some companies to us?"

Selena liked the sound of this. She wondered if last night was the reason why Justin had changed his mind. "We can forward you a list. Pedro, you have just added on to your bookstore."

"Yes, I did and I'm very pleased with the work I had done. That is great for the construction companies, Cam, but what about the business owners who are already in the marketplace?" Pedro asked.

"We will be using the existing vendors for the most part but we will be redesigning the stores," Justin said entering the room.

He had been outside today—his tan was deeper. He was dressed the same way he'd been when he left her this morning and it felt like it had been longer than eight hours since she'd seen him.

"We don't want slick-looking new stores," Tomas said.

"I will be consulting with each of you individually. I'd like to schedule meetings over the next few days to figure out what you think will work and for us to consult with you. Then hopefully you will lift your protest and we can get to work."

"We'll see," Selena said. "Justin, do you have the requests for bid?"

"I do," he said, handing them to her.

She glanced down at the forms and skimmed them. "Can I have a few minutes to meet with the committee without you guys?"

"Sure," Cam said.

The two men left the boardroom and Selena stood up and looked at her grandfather and the other men and women she'd grown up with. "I think we are in a position to get what we want if we handle this carefully. No one can be thrown out of their business due to the constraint that another local must be brought in if they don't renew your lease."

"That's good news. Now how do we keep the Cuban American feel in this new development?" Tomas asked.

"How many of you have been to Luna Azul?"

A few hands were raised but not enough. "Tonight's assignment, folks, is to go check out your enemy. I want you to visit the downstairs club to see the kind of effort they have put into redoing the building, but I think you will all be impressed by what they've created on their rooftop club. That's the kind of ambiance and feeling I want to see them bring to the Mercado."

"What do you mean by that? I can't take your *abuelita* to a night club."

"It's not a night club like you are thinking, *abuelito*. And you have to do it. Then we will all meet tomorrow… can we use your bookstore again, Pedro?"

"*Si*, that sounds good to me."

"They are going to build their marketplace no matter how many obstacles we put up. We just have to ensure they build it the way we want it," Selena said.

There were a chorus of murmurs around the table but everyone agreed to go to Luna Azul that night. "Will you be there?" Tomas asked.

"I checked out the club earlier. And I have plans tonight," she said.

"With who?" her grandfather asked.

"None of your business," she said.

"It must be a man," Pedro said.

"Never you mind," Pedro's wife Luz said. "She told you to keep your nose out of it."

"I am. It's just not like our Selena to have a date."

And this was why she lived several states away from these people. She knew they loved her and cared about her but she didn't like having her entire life discussed in a committee meeting.

"Okay, that's it. I'm going to go and get the Stern

brothers and tell them we should be ready to meet with them again early next week."

"That works for me," Pedro said and soon everyone else agreed. The other business owners left and Selena's grandfather kissed her before following them out.

He paused on the threshold of the conference room. "Come for breakfast tomorrow so we can talk."

"Abuelito—"

"No arguments, *tata*. I want to know about this man you are seeing."

"You don't have to worry about him being like Raul."

"I'm not, *tata*. The fact that you are being so secretive tells me that you're worried, though."

"Fine, but I'm coming for lunch, not breakfast."

"Agreed."

She stood there watching him walk away. Realizing that he was entirely correct—she was afraid of letting Justin in because she knew deep down that love was a losing game, at least where she was concerned.

Ten

It had been a long day, Justin thought as he drove through the quiet tree-lined neighborhood to Selena's house. The buildings around here were relatively new since this area had been hit hard by Hurricane Andrew back in '92 and completely rebuilt.

He felt good about all he'd accomplished today. Normally at this point in a negotiation he'd be chomping at the bit to close the deal, but this time he knew as soon as everyone was happy, Selena was out of here and that was the last thing he wanted.

Her suggestion that the Luna Azul Mercado committee go to the club tonight was genius. Nate and Cam were going to ensure they all had a good time; Nate had even invited his good friend, the rapper and movie star Hutch Damien, to join them. Nate's fiancée Jen Miller was going to teach them all a few salsa steps and use them for the opening conga line.

He pulled to a stop in the driveway of the address that Selena had given him. She was going to cook him a traditional Cuban meal.

He rubbed the back of his neck and sighed. As far as business decisions went, his being here wasn't his best. That was it. He could tell himself that he was doing this to blow off steam or to learn his enemy a little better but at the end of the day he knew he was here for one reason and one reason only.

He wanted to be.

Selena was changing him. And he knew that she didn't want to and was probably not even aware she was doing it. She had her own agenda and her own secrets. Secrets he was determined to find out tonight.

The front door opened and she stepped out onto the small porch. She was barefoot and wore a pair of khaki Bermuda shorts and a patterned wraparound shirt.

"Are you going to come in or just sit out here all night?" she asked.

"Oh, I'm coming in," he said, pushing the button to put the top up on his car and gathering the flowers and wine he'd brought for her.

Though his parents' relationship wasn't the best, his father had always said that you don't go to visit a woman empty-handed.

He came up her walkway noticing that the lawn was well kept but rather plain. There were no flowers in the beds at the front of the house and compared to her neighbors, this house seemed a little...lonely.

As did Selena as she stood there on her porch with one arm wrapped around her waist. She stepped inside as he came toward her and he followed her into the tiled foyer, which was done in deep, rich earth tones in a Spanish design.

As they headed farther into the sparsely furnished house, the walls were painted a muted yellow. There was a family portrait hanging in a position of prominence in her formal living room and the dining room was to the right.

"Whose house is this?" he asked.

"Mine," she said.

"Where you grew up?" he asked.

"No. I…I inherited it from my great-aunt. I usually rent it out and give my grandparents the income from it. But since I was back in town, my *abuelita* didn't book anyone for this summer."

"So why are you staying at the Ritz instead of here?" he asked. This home was warm and welcoming, though he could tell that she didn't live in it. There was a formal feeling that didn't fit with the Selena he'd come to know.

"I just…there are ghosts of the past here and I really want to focus on doing my job and going back to New York. Besides I can't pretend to be on vacation if I'm staying here."

"Fair enough," he said. "I brought these for you."

He handed her the flowers, which she raised to her nose to sniff. The bouquet held roses and white daisies.

"Lovely," she said without looking up from the flowers. "I'm going to put them in water. Want to come in the kitchen with me? Or you can wait outside back by the pool."

"I'll stay with you," he said, following her through the living room into the eat-in kitchen, which was made for entertaining. There was a breakfast bar with two stools and place settings. She walked around and opened a cabinet to find a vase and put the flowers in water. Then she leaned on the counter and looked at him.

"Thank you. I think my dad was the last man to give me flowers."

He knew her parents were dead so that meant it had been too long since a man had treated Selena right.

"You are very welcome," he said, putting the bottle of red wine on the counter.

"Dinner's almost ready. I thought we could have a drink and sit outside by the pool," she said.

"Sounds perfect to me," he said. She mixed them both mojitos and then led the way out to the pool deck. There was a fountain in the center of the traditional rectangular pool. She sat down on one of the large padded loungers and he took a seat next to her.

"So…how did things go today with my brother?" he asked. "Why didn't you mention your meeting was with him?"

"Probably the same reason you didn't tell me you were golfing with Maxwell this morning."

He laughed at that. "I guess we both are doing what we have to in order to win."

"Indeed. One thing I observed at the club today was a true love and appreciation of Cuban American society and history."

"We are definitely indebted to the community, which is why we want to make the marketplace the best it can be."

"I can see that. Your brother told me about your nanny."

"Maria? She was a great storyteller. She had a gift for making everything she said seem real."

"My papa was like that. He'd tell me grand stories before bed every night about a tiny girl who would fly to the moon and the adventures she'd have there." Selena smiled to herself. "He made me feel invincible."

Justin sat on the edge of his chair facing her. "What or who made you realize you weren't?"

Selena didn't want to talk about her past but with Justin she knew she would. Normally, she didn't date. That was pretty much how she'd avoided talking about her family and Raul for the last ten years. She'd had some casual boyfriends but those relationships had been brief, defined by their jobs and busy schedules.

Being back in Miami had awakened something long dead inside of her and she knew that she wasn't going to be able to just shrug this off.

"It's a long story and not very flattering," she said.

"I'm listening," he said. "Not judging."

She was glad to hear that but it didn't make finding the right words any easier. In her head were all the details, she knew the facts about what happened but she realized that she'd never had to really talk about them out loud.

"You are the first person I've attempted to tell this to," she said.

"I'm flattered."

She shrugged. "I'm not really sure I can talk about it now."

"This is the reason that your grandparents sold the marketplace?" he asked. He'd respected her privacy and stayed away from digging into her past on his own. He trusted her to tell him. Selena was nothing if not a woman of her word and he'd come to really respect her during the time they'd spent together.

"Yes, it is. I guess I'm making this into something more than it really is...I fell in love with a con man and it took a lot of money to make him go away. My *abuelito* went to the cops and they set up a sting to capture Raul—that's the man I was conned by—and he eventually was arrested and convicted. I made sure my grandparents got their money back but it took too long for them to buy back the marketplace."

He took a deep breath as anger exploded inside at the way she'd been treated. He was glad that Tomas had had the foresight to make sure that the man who'd hurt her had been caught and prosecuted.

He didn't want to say the wrong thing but he was so angry that a man had betrayed her love that way. He could scarcely sit still. He stood up and paced around, wanting to do something to make it right.

"I don't know what to say. This isn't what I expected to hear from you about your past."

"I'm not the girl I used to be. I don't…I don't get involved with men on such a deep level anymore. It happened right after my parents died."

"That bastard took advantage of you when you were vulnerable," he said.

He got out of his lounger and scooped her up into his arms before sitting back down on her chair and cradling her. "You are a very strong woman, Selena. I think you should take great pride in the fact that an event that could have made you bitter and resentful instead made you stronger."

She tipped her head up to look him in the eyes and he realized it would be so easy to get lost in her big brown orbs. "Do you mean that?"

"You know I don't say things I don't mean."

"That is true," she said. "You shoot straight from the hip, don't you?" She smiled and gently stroked his cheek.

He smiled at her because he knew she wanted to lighten this moment but it didn't change the fact that he was still angry on her behalf and he wanted answers. He wanted to make sure the person who hurt her never came near her again. Make sure that she was never hurt again. Make sure that she was protected.

The intensity of his feelings surprised him. But a few minutes later when she told him she had to go check on dinner, he finally let her go. He sat there by her pool realizing that no matter how much he'd been trying to tell himself that she wasn't going to matter to him, she did. Selena wasn't just his vacation fling; she meant more.

He should have acknowledged that from the beginning. He didn't flirt in waiting rooms or go out of his way to date women he had business dealings with. She was different.

She called him to dinner a few minutes later and they ate at her patio table with soft music coming from the intercom. He tried to keep the conversation light but it was harder than he'd thought it would be.

"I guess you are looking at me differently now," she said as they finished their meal.

He nodded. "Yes, I am. I'm sorry but I wish that I had five minutes alone with that bastard Raul."

"I shouldn't have told you," she said.

"You needed to," he said. "If you have never talked about it until now, then it was past time. Have you been back to Miami since everything happened?"

"For Enrique's high school graduation. But I flew in on a Friday night and out on Sunday morning. I didn't really have time to do anything but marvel over the fact that my baby brother had grown up."

"So how does it feel being in Miami this time

around?" Justin asked. "I guess that you're ready to deal with it."

She shrugged delicately and looked away from him. "I thought so…actually that's a lie. I figured what happened ten years ago wouldn't bother me anymore. But being here…dealing with you and knowing that if I hadn't fallen for Raul's sweet lies my grandparents wouldn't have to be negotiating with your company for their livelihood, well that forced me to face the fact that this is all my doing."

"I don't think it's that bad. Your grandparents don't blame you for anything and I know you are smart enough to realize now that Luna Azul isn't the devil."

She tipped her head to the side studying him. "I'm not sure. I fell for a smooth-talking man once and I don't want to make the same mistake again. Especially since it will be my grandparents who pay the price once again."

He didn't like the fact that she'd put him in the same category as a con man. "I've never lied to you and I'm not trying to cheat you or your grandparents out of anything. I resent the fact that you said that."

Selena rubbed the back of her neck. The last thing she'd intended to do was to offend him, but he had to understand that she was trying to protect herself.

"I didn't mean to say that you were swindling me or my grandparents," she said.

"Yes, you did. You wanted to make sure that I understood that you don't trust me."

"You? It has nothing to do with you," she said. She wasn't thinking, just reacting, and she realized she was being truer with Justin than she'd been with any man before. "I don't trust men. That's it, period, end of story.

I want to believe you when you say you are dealing honestly with me, but then I find out you are meeting with the zoning commissioner behind my back."

"Maxwell and I are friends. And you did the same thing to me. Going to meet my brother. What did you think that Cam would do, offer you better terms?" he asked.

An argument was brewing and she knew she was responsible for it. She'd simply wanted to tell him that trusting him wasn't easy for her and now she'd somehow gotten them into a mess that she had no idea how to get out of.

"I thought he'd give me some insight into whether he was the same kind of man you are. The kind of man I can trust. Because you aren't the only Stern brother that my grandparents and the other business owners are going to have to deal with."

He leaned back in his chair. "Damn, I'm sorry I got a little hot under the collar."

"A little? That's an understatement."

He shook his head. "You make me passionate, so of course I'm upset that you'd lump me in the same category as a guy who'd bilk your grandparents out of their fortune."

"I'm sorry about that. I didn't mean it that way," she said, then paused. "Do I really make you passionate?" she asked.

"Hell, yes. I know we just broke our number one rule about not talking about business when we are alone—"

"That was a stupid idea. I can't keep up two lives. I mean it would be nice to think that I could do it but to be honest I feel too much when I'm here. And it's clear to me you do, too."

"Yes, I do. In the spirit of open communication, I knew I wouldn't be able to think clearly unless I got the passion I felt for you out of my system."

"Oh, really?" she asked, getting up and coming around to his side of the table. He scooted his chair out and pulled her down on his lap.

"Yes, really."

She toyed with his collar, caressing the exposed skin of his neck. "Is it working?"

"Not yet. The more I get to know about you, Selena, the more I need to know. I feel like I will never be able to know enough about you and that's not acceptable. I never let anyone have that much control over me."

"So I can control you?" she asked, trying to keep things flirty and light because otherwise she was going to have to face the fact that Justin was more of a man than any other guy she'd ever let into her life.

For one thing, he was willing to admit that this was confusing him as much as it was confusing her. That shouldn't turn her on, but it did. It made her want to wrap her entire body around his and make love to him here on her patio. But she wasn't going to do that. She couldn't.

Already he was starting to become more important to her than she'd expected him to be. She had to remember that she was leaving in a few weeks.

"About as much as I can control you," he said. His hands settled on her waist and she looked down into his eyes.

There was something so pure about the color of his eyes and she felt like she could get lost in them. Get lost in the life that she once had and the life that she'd always dreamed of having. Dreams that had been swept away by Raul's actions.

"I'm afraid," she admitted in a soft whisper and put her head down on his shoulder.

"Afraid of what?" he asked, his hands moving smoothly over her back.

She didn't know if she could put it into words but then the simple truth was there. "You…me. I guess I'm scared of the way you make me feel. I've been so focused on my career and I've found a way to live with the past and with my mistakes. But now you are making me want again."

"Wanting is good," he said.

She turned her head on his shoulder and kissed his neck. "Wanting is very good. But I'm afraid that it is changing me. I thought I knew who I was. I thought that the woman I'd once been was completely gone but being back here has made me realize I'm not sure who I am."

He tipped her head back so that he could look down in her eyes. "You know who you are, you just didn't want to admit that there was still a part of you that could be passionate about a man and about this place."

She leaned up and kissed him hard on the lips. "Why do you think that?"

"Because it's in your eyes. I don't see a woman who doubts herself at all."

"I'm not talking about confidence," she said.

"What are you talking about then?"

"I'm talking about dreams," she said. "I thought that I was the kind of woman who would be happy with a career and a life in the big city…not the city of my childhood but a new place. A place where I'd carved out my own life. But I think I just realized that I haven't been living."

"You haven't?" he asked.

She shook her head, letting her hair brush over his hands as she leaned forward and kissed him gently. No matter what else came from her time with Justin she'd always be grateful to him for making her realize what had been missing in her life.

"No, I've been hiding and I'm just now realizing that I let Raul steal something from me. And you, Justin Stern, my *abuelito's* silver-tongued devil, are slowly giving it back to me."

Eleven

Justin carried Selena back over to the lounger where he'd held her earlier. He'd had enough of talking. What he needed was something that made sense to him. Something he didn't have to dissect and analyze. He needed to have her body, naked and writhing, under him.

He needed them both to get out of their heads and he needed that right now. He lowered her onto the lounger and sat next to her hip.

"What are you doing?"

"If you can't figure it out then I'm not doing it correctly."

She shook her head. "It feels like lovemaking."

"Then that's what it is," he said. "I was hoping you'd say it felt like an erotic dream come true."

"It's more than that. Last night was so much more than I thought I'd find with a man…"

"That's what I wanted to hear," he said.

"I'm glad. I didn't expect to like you."

"Same here. But I knew from the moment I sat down next to you in the zoning office that you were different."

She smiled up at him. "Really. I thought you were just this crazy guy who thought with his libido instead of his head."

She made him feel good and happy, he thought. It didn't matter what the future held at this moment—he was more relaxed and turned on than he'd ever been.

He reached for the tie that seemed to hold her blouse together and undid it. He pulled the fabric open and found there was a little button on the inside that still had to be unfastened. But he was distracted from getting her completely naked by the one breast he had already uncovered.

She wore a nude colored mesh bra that was almost like a second skin. He growled low in his throat and caressed the full globe of that revealed breast, moving his fingers up to her nipple. "I love this bra."

"I'm glad. I wore it for you."

"What else did you wear for me?"

"Why don't you make yourself comfortable and I'll show you?" She stood up and he moved so he was lying back on the lounger. Selena was innately sensual and despite what she'd said about not knowing who she was, he knew she was one of the most confident women he'd ever met. There was something very sure about her, as she slowly removed her blouse and dropped it on the other chair.

"So you like this?" she asked cupping her breasts and leaning forward.

"Very much." Not touching her was torture but he

was determined to let her have this moment. And to let her seduce him.

She put her hands to her waistband and slowly lowered the zipper. Through the opening in her shorts he saw her smooth stomach and belly button before she slowly parted the cloth.

"I'm not sure you really want to see this," she said.

"Trust me, I do."

"Then take off your shirt."

"Show me a little something and I'll consider it."

She turned around and swiveled her hips at him. She lowered the fabric of her shorts the tiniest bit so that he saw the indentation at the small of her back and the thin nude colored elastic at the waist of her panties.

"Whatcha got for me, Justin?"

He stood up; being passive wasn't in his nature. He toed off his loafers and started unbuttoning his shirt. He let it hang open as he came up behind her. He wrapped his arms around her waist and bent to taste the side of her neck.

"This is what I have for you," he said. Taking her hips in his hands and drawing her back until her buttocks was nestled against his erection. He rubbed up and down against her.

She shivered delicately and tossed her hair as she turned her head to look back at him. "That's exactly what I need."

"I'm glad," he said, nibbling against her skin as he talked. He moved his hands over her stomach, feeling the bare skin. He dipped his finger in her belly button and her hips swiveled against his.

He pushed hands lower into the opening of her shorts and cupped her feminine mound in his hand. She was humid and hot and she shifted herself against his palm.

He pressed against her and she swiveled her hips again, this time caressing him.

He loved the feel of her against his erection. He pushed her pants down her legs and then reached between them to open his own pants and free himself.

He groaned when he felt the naked globes of her ass against his erection. She had on a thong.

"God, woman, you are killing me," he rasped in her ear.

"Good. I have thought of nothing else but you and me like this since you dropped me off this morning."

"Me, too," he admitted. He kept caressing her between her legs and used his other hand to push the thin piece of fabric that guarded her secrets out of the way.

She moaned his name and parted her legs, shifting forward so that he could enter her more smoothly. He held her hips with both of his hands as he pushed up inside her. He started moving, listening to the sounds she made.

He loved her sex noises and had a feeling he'd never tire of hearing them. Her velvety smooth walls contracted around him with each thrust he made. He felt his orgasm getting closer with each thrust into her body.

Everything started tingling, and then he erupted with a deep pulse. He heard her cry out as he emptied himself into her. She slumped forward in his arms and it took all of his strength to keep them on their feet. As soon as he was able to, he pulled out and lifted her in his arms, carrying her into the house.

"Where's your bathroom?" he asked. She liked the way that sex roughened his voice and made it low and raspy. At this moment she felt like the other things she spent all day worrying about didn't really matter.

"Down the hall, first door on the left."

He carried her down the hall, but she hardly paid attention to any of it. Just kept her head on his shoulder and thought about how nice it was to have a big strong man to carry her. It wasn't that she couldn't take care of herself because she could; it was that she didn't have to do anything right now.

She felt safe and…cherished. That was it. She'd never experienced it before. He made her feel like she was the most important person in his world at this moment. And she wasn't going to allow herself to analyze it and dissect it and figure out why she shouldn't just enjoy it.

He set her on the counter. Her bathroom had a large garden tub with spa jets. He turned the tap and adjusted the temperature.

He was a very fine-looking man. She'd be happy to watch him move around naked all day long.

"Bubble bath?" he asked.

"Under the sink. I can get it," she started to hop down.

"No, stay where you are. I want to do this for you," he said, standing up and coming over to her. Wrapped his arms around her waist and tugged her close to him for a hug.

She rested her head against his chest and had the fleeting sensation that this wasn't going to last. Like she should hold on to him as tight as she could right now. She squeezed him to her and he pulled back.

"You okay?"

"Yeah. Ready for this bath."

"Me, too."

He found the bubble bath and poured it into the running water. Soon there was a sea of bubbles as he turned the faucet off. He lifted her up and then stepped into the tub.

He sat down in the water, which was the perfect temperature, and cradled her on his lap.

"Are you okay?"

"Yes, why wouldn't I be?" she asked.

"I was like an animal out there. You turned me on and I couldn't think of anything except having you. Damn, just thinking about it is getting me hard again," he said.

"I thought men of a certain age took a little longer to recover," she said.

"Not with you around," he admitted. He pulled her back against her, moving his hands over her body.

"Why aren't you staying here?" he asked after a moment. "The real reason."

"I told you…it doesn't feel like home," she said. "And to be honest every time I'm here I remember all the bad things that happened. It makes me feel guilty and sad."

He hugged her close, and he was so sweet in that moment that she felt her heart start to melt. She knew she couldn't give in to that and let herself start to care for him—hell, who was she kidding, she already cared for him or she wouldn't have cooked for him. She was starting to fall for him and that was more dangerous than anything else she could do.

"I hope you will be thinking of me in this place now," he said.

"I definitely will be," she said. And that was a big part of her problem. He was slowly making himself a part of her time here. Making her want to stay in the one place she vowed she'd never make her home again.

They finished their bath with lots of caressing and

touching and Selena felt very mellow after they dried off. She found the dressing gowns that her grandmother kept in the closet for guests who rented the house and they put them on. He led her back outside to the pool and she wasn't surprised when he offered to clean up the dinner dishes for her.

"You don't have to do that. Why don't you mix us some drinks while I take care of those," she said.

He went to the bar, stopping along the way to pick up his cell phone. She suspected he was checking his email and she didn't like it. It was like he was going back to the businessman he essentially was.

She wondered if the sweet guy stuff was an act. Was that part of how he was playing her to make sure that she went along with all of his suggestions?

She piled their dinner dishes on a tray and took them inside to the kitchen putting them away before rejoining Justin.

When she got out on the patio, Justin had put his pants back on and was buttoning his shirt.

"I'm sorry but something has come up and I have to go."

She nodded. "No problem."

He stared at her for a minute. "Okay, good. So I will see you in a couple of days to start our meetings with the tenants of the marketplace."

"Sure."

It felt to her like he was running away and she didn't want to let it upset her but it did. It bothered her that she'd spent the evening with him, seduced him and shared the secrets of her past with him and now he was running out the door as fast as he could.

"I wish I could stay," he said.

"It's not a big deal," she replied. If he truly wanted to stay he'd stay.

"It is. Listen, I can't ignore this page," he said. "Are you spending the night here or at the hotel?"

"The hotel, why?"

"Let's meet for a nightcap. Say, eleven?"

"Why?" she asked again.

"I don't want you to think I'm the kind of man who runs away."

She wrapped her arm around her waist and then realized what it was she was doing and dropped it. "I don't know what kind of man you are."

"Yes, you do," he said. "I will remind you when I see you later tonight."

He kissed her hard on the lips and walked through her house and out the front door.

Justin didn't have an emergency waiting for him—he was a businessman not a surgeon—but he'd had to get out of there. Had to breathe and remind himself that as far as Selena was concerned they were having a vacation affair.

And he needed to remember that. He wasn't looking for the future Mrs. Justin Stern. He wasn't getting married ever and if he did change his mind…well, that wasn't going to happen, at least not now.

He drove aimlessly, finding himself in the parking lot of Luna Azul. Sitting in his car he wondered why he was still here. Cam didn't need him in Miami to continue helping to run the company. Not like he had in the beginning when they'd all three bonded together and did every job they could themselves to cut costs.

He could be anywhere else he wanted to, even New

York. But he knew he wouldn't leave. He couldn't leave. This place was in his blood. This was home.

Someone knocked on his window and he glanced up to see Nate standing there. He turned off the car engine and got out.

"What are you doing?"

"Thinking."

"I guess I can see why you were alone. Takes all your concentration, right?"

"Ha."

"Ha? Damn, man, you don't sound like yourself. What's up?"

He shook his head. No way was he going to tell his little brother that he was confused and a woman was responsible. Nate would laugh himself into a stupor if Justin admitted such a thing.

"Do you ever miss baseball?"

Nate shrugged his muscled shoulders. "Some days, but I don't dwell on it. It's not like I'm going to ever be able to go back."

"What about that high school coach from Texas who made the majors in his forties?"

"He was a pitcher, Jus. I'm not. Plus I like this life. I don't know that I'd be committed enough to work out every day and do all the traveling," Nate said then tipped his head to the side. "Besides, you'd miss me."

Justin smiled at his little brother. "I would. I never thought we'd all end up working together."

"I didn't either, but I bet Cam knew," Nate said.

"What are you doing out here?"

"I …I have a date."

"With Jen? I thought you were engaged, so dating was a thing of the past."

"She likes it when we meet up after she gets done with work and then we have a little alone time."

"Alone time? Seriously. You crack me up," Justin said but to be honest he was envious of his brother and his fiancée. Until this moment he hadn't realized that he wanted what Nate had found. And he knew it was because of Selena.

"I still have to head out after our 'date' to schmooze more celebs but this gives us a little time together."

"Sounds nice," Justin admitted.

"Thanks, bro. So are you going inside?"

"No. I have to head back to my office. I want to review some notes I made earlier."

"At this time of the night? I know Cam is a bit of a pain about this marketplace project but I think he'd let you have a night off."

"You know he doesn't want me to take any time until this is all wrapped up."

Nate arched one eyebrow at him. "You're not big on vacations."

"No, I'm not. I'm a workaholic so I guess it shouldn't surprise you that I'm heading to the office."

"Normally no, but I've never caught you sitting in the parking lot before."

Justin realized that his brother was now concerned. "I'm just looking at all we've accomplished."

"It always makes me proud, too," Nate said, glancing at his watch. "I've got to get inside. I'm hosting that group from the marketplace for drinks after the last show and I don't want to be late to meet with Jen."

"Don't let me keep you. I'm heading to my office."

Justin hugged his brother and then got back in his car and drove away. He needed to pay attention to the deal with the Luna Azul Mercado and get that finalized. Then he'd figure out what to do with Selena.

He wasn't going to allow her to continue to control him the way she had tonight. The only thing that made her power over him acceptable was the fact that she seemed unaware of it.

He pulled into the parking lot of their office building and didn't want to get out. For the first time in his adult life he wasn't interested in working. In fact, only one thing was on his mind and it was Selena.

He'd been an idiot to leave when he had. What had he proved?

He realized he'd proved to himself that he could be the one to leave.

And that was important. His father had never been able to leave their mother and that had been his greatest flaw. It had made the old man weak and Justin had decided at a very young age that he wasn't going to be like his old man. At least not when it came to love.

He wasn't going to fall for the wrong kind of woman. To be honest he'd vowed to never let any woman mean more to him than business.

He forced himself to get out of the car and go up to his office. He spent two hours going over numbers and sending detailed notes to his assistant for the meetings they'd be having over the next few days. By the time he'd left the office, he knew he was a much stronger man than his father had ever been and that Selena Gonzalez wasn't going to find the same flaw in him that his mother had found in his father.

Twelve

Selena changed her outfit about six times but finally went down to the lobby bar a little after eleven. If Justin weren't there, she'd know he was a bit of a con man just like Raul had been. But instead of going after her grandparents' money, Justin was going after—what?

That was the question she didn't know how to answer. She was pretty sure he wasn't after her heart, which she'd like to know more about. She knew most men were commitment-phobes but he took it to extremes, from what she'd observed.

Why then was she standing at the entrance to the mood-lit bar so tentatively? Hoping for...

Justin.

He'd come. To be honest, until she saw him she'd been afraid to hope that he would be here. She just had figured he wouldn't show up.

He waved her over to the intimate banquette where

he was sitting. She sat down and slid around the bench until she was next to him.

He leaned over and kissed her cheek. He'd had time to go and change and he'd put on aftershave but he hadn't shaved because a five o'clock shadow darkened his jaw.

She didn't to talk about the way he'd left. She'd spent most of the night reliving those moments and trying to ascertain if it had been something she'd done.

"Business emergency handled?"

He flushed and nodded. "It wasn't a big deal—just some paperwork that needed signing."

That didn't sound like a reason for him to rush out of her house but she wasn't going to call him on it. She'd see how the rest of the evening went and then make up her mind if he was playing her for a fool or just in over his head like she was.

But Justin didn't seem like the type of man to be overwhelmed by anything.

"What do you want to drink? They make a nice Irish coffee here, but I've always been partial to cognac."

"Me, too," she said. "My *abuelito* used to pour me a small snifter after I turned sixteen to share with him on Sundays when we'd go over to his house for dinner. I always felt very grown-up drinking it."

"My dad always had cigars with cognac, but I don't think we can smoke in here."

"Not at all. Do you smoke?" she asked, realizing that she really didn't know him all too well.

"No. I mean, the occasional cigar. When we first opened Luna Azul it was right at the height of the cigar club phase and we toyed with making it one, but in the end we wanted something that would stay in fashion."

"Good call."

"It was Nate who pointed out it was a fad. That guy has his finger on the pulse of what's hot and what's not."

"I would imagine so—I see him on the society page of the newspaper almost every day."

Justin signaled the waiter and ordered their drinks. "Nate does a lot of that socializing for the club. We get a lot of tourists and locals in the club because they want to catch a glimpse of Nate and his A-list friends."

"I noticed that you and your brothers are close, what about your parents?" she asked. She wanted to know everything about him, the personal stuff that she hadn't thought was important before. She knew from Cam that his parents were gone but she wanted to know more about the brothers' relationship with them.

"My parents are both dead."

"I know—Cam told me. I'm sorry. I know how it is to lose your parents."

"It wasn't that bad. I had a little bit of high school left and Cam stepped in to fill the void."

"I guess you weren't that close to them, then," she said.

"No, I wasn't. Well, my dad. He always took my brothers and I out all the time."

"Where did he take you? Were you rough-and-tumble boys?" she asked.

"He mainly took us to the golf course or out on his boat. Just out of the house. My mother was often socializing and didn't want noisy boys in the way."

It didn't really sound bitter when he said it but she was surprised and a little hurt for him. "My mother loved having us in the house and under her feet. My brother is ten years younger than I was so to keep me from being lonely my mom would always have my cousins over for me to play with," Selena said, remembering the crazy games she used to play with her cousins and how much fun it had been.

"My brothers and I are all two years apart, I guess it was too much for my mother. My dad enjoyed having us with him. I think we learned about living from him."

Their drinks arrived.

"Salud!" she said raising her glass toward him.

"Cheers," he replied.

They both took a sip of their drinks. She set her glass on the table in front of her.

"What did you think of your dad being a pro golfer?"

"Why are you asking me so many questions?"

She didn't know how to answer that. The truth was it had hurt when he left and she wanted to figure out what made him tick so he'd never hurt her again. Frankly, there was no way she was going to tell him that. "You know my family but I really don't know much about yours."

"Fair enough."

"What was your dad's name?"

"Kurt Stern."

"I've never heard of him."

"Most people who aren't very familiar with golf haven't. But he made a very good living playing for all of his life. He and my mother were killed when their private plane crashed on the way to a golf tournament."

Suddenly she did know who his father was. She remembered reading the story about the tragedy. "Of course. I remember seeing that in the news."

"I should have led with that part. He was more famous in death than he was in life."

"I'm sorry I didn't realize who he was."

He took her hand in his. "It's okay. Most people don't."

Justin felt like today had gone on too long. He was ready for it to end but not ready to leave Selena. Yet he knew he'd have to. Spending the night with her when they were on his yacht was one thing, spending the night with her here at the hotel something else. He just wasn't ready for it tonight. He didn't trust himself.

"Thanks for meeting for this drink," he said.

"I guess you are done talking about your family?"

"Way done. I don't like to talk about the past. I prefer to look to the future, which we are doing with our partnership."

"Which one?"

That was the question. "The Mercado is what brought us together."

"That is so true. If my *abuelito* hadn't thought you were a silver-tongued devil our paths never would have crossed."

He frowned as he realized how right she was. It had been chance that had put their paths on a collision course. "I guess it was fate."

She smirked. "Only if you count me falling for Raul as part of fate's ultimate plan. And I'm not sure that our destinies are that spelled out."

He wasn't either. "I've made everything in my life happen by hard work and determination, so I'd have to agree with you."

"Still…for me it would be reassuring if I thought all the heartache and trouble with Raul was so that my grandparents could have an even better place now. I mean that would be worth it."

He wondered if she thought he'd be worth it. What was the man of her dreams? Or had those died when she'd been twenty and betrayed by love? Tonight wasn't the night for asking that type of question.

"It would be worth it. I hope you know it was never my intent to swindle anyone out of anything."

"I think I do know that now. At first I wasn't too sure what to think of you."

"Why?"

She took a deep breath and then leaned forward, crossing her arms on the table. Her arms framed her breasts—he tried to keep his gaze on her face but he was distracted. He liked this woman. He loved her body and he wanted nothing more than to spend every night wrapped in her arms.

"I guess it was the way you came on to me. I thought 'this guy has got to be after something.'"

"Selena," he said, taking her hands in his and looking into those deep chocolate-colored eyes of hers. "I was after you. I didn't know who you were when we were sitting next to each other. I only knew that I wanted you."

"Lust," she said. "The mighty Justin Stern was floored by lust."

He squeezed her hand and lifted it to his lips to kiss the back of it. "I wasn't floored."

"Oh, what were you then?"

"Enamored. I had never seen a woman as beautiful as you," he said, meaning those words more than any he'd ever spoken before. There was something about Selena that struck him deep in his soul. He wasn't the kind of man who made soul connections or thought he'd find his other half but a part of him—the part that had run away from her house earlier—knew that he had. That there was something between the two of them that just couldn't be stopped.

"It was a force of nature," he said.

"You do have a silver tongue."

He didn't like that she thought so. "I don't. I'm known for being blunt and to the point. There is something about you that has captivated me."

"I wish I could believe you," she said, her eyes big and almost sad.

"Why can't you?"

"Men—"

He knew she was going to make a blanket statement that wouldn't be flattering. He knew he should let it go, it was late, they both had a full day of meetings tomorrow and to be fair she'd let him escape her house earlier without asking too many questions. But he wanted to know what she thought of men. Wanted to know the exact company he was keeping.

"Men what?"

"Some men lie. And they do it so well that a person never knows that they aren't telling the truth," she said. She shook her head. "I'm sorry, Justin. I wish I was a different woman who didn't have baggage."

"I don't," he said. He knew she'd been badly used and that the effect was one she still hadn't shaken. Raul's betrayal wasn't just of Selena and her heart but also of her family and he suspected that hurt her even more.

"Why not?"

"You wouldn't be the woman you are today without the past."

She leaned over and hugged him. "Thanks for saying just the right thing."

"Ha, I knew if I blundered around long enough I'd come off as suave."

"I didn't say you were suave."

"You implied it," he said. "I think we should call it a night before you change your mind."

She nibbled on her lower lip and he wondered if she was hesitating over tonight the way he was. When she didn't offer for him to come up to her room, he realized she was just as shy about where this was heading.

"I've got an early meeting so maybe we could have lunch?"

She shook her head. "I can't. I'm due to be grilled by my grandparents for lunch."

"Grilled about what?"

"You. Everyone on the committee guessed I had a date since I didn't come with them to the club and now I'm being called back home to answer for myself."

"Are you going to tell them your date was with me?" he asked.

"Definitely, I'm not lying to them."

"Would you like me to come with you?" he asked.

"That's sweet but I think I better handle this one alone."

"Very well, but let's meet for breakfast."

She nodded and they went their separate ways at the elevator. He down to his suite and she down to hers. He felt like he'd created a barrier between them tonight by running away. And as he fell asleep he realized that he wanted her in his arms. He needed her in his arms and he was going to make sure she was back there as soon as possible.

Selena woke up with the sun streaming through the windows and her thoughts on Justin. He knocked on her door at seven-thirty and she was surprised to see he wore his robe and was pushing a room service cart.

"This is as close as I could get to breakfast in bed, considering that you didn't invite me to spend the night," he said.

"You didn't seem like you were interested," she said.

"My mistake," he said, pulling her into his arms. He walked her back toward the bed.

He didn't say anything but pulled her under him. His robe fell open and he shrugged it off his shoulders revealing his nakedness. He pushed her nightgown up to her waist and slid into her body. He rocked them slowly together.

The sensation of having him inside of her again was exquisite.

She'd grown accustomed to his touch and it felt right to have him here between her legs. In her again. She no longer felt like she was alone.

She knew she was drawn to the feel of him. His body under her fingers, his chest rubbing against her breasts and the feel of his mouth on her neck with that early morning stubble abrading her. She shivered as he whispered darkly sexual words against her skin and rocked his hips leisurely against hers.

The first time they'd made love had been intense and explosive, the second time sweet and sensual, but this morning it felt like coming home. She was awash in feelings of Justin as they slowly moved together.

She scraped her nails down his back until she could cup his butt and pull him closer to her. He paused buried hilt-deep inside of her.

He lifted his head and looked down at her. "Good morning."

"Yes, it is," she said, feeling more relaxed than she

had in a long time. There was something nice about making love first thing in the morning.

"I like the feel of your hands on me."

"Me, too," she admitted. "From the moment I saw you in the lobby of the zoning office I wanted to touch your butt."

He gave her a wicked smile. "I wanted to touch your breasts."

He lowered his head and took the tip of one of her nipples between his lips, suckling her softly in the early morning light.

His hands moved over the sides of her torso and he cupped her other breast in his hand then rotated his palm over it. Stimulating it until the nipple hardened.

She shifted her shoulders as he started to suckle more strongly. She put her heels on the bed trying to get him to move in her but he wouldn't be budged. This morning he was determined to take his time and drive her slowly out of her mind.

"Please…"

"Please what? Doesn't this feel good?"

"Yes, it feels too good," she said.

"How can something feel too good?" he asked, tracing the edge of her areola with his tongue.

She couldn't think. The humid warmth of his tongue contrasted with the slight abrasion of his stubble and it was driving her mad.

"Just please…"

"Please what?" he asked.

"Make love to me," she said at last, looking into those clear blue eyes of his.

"My pleasure," he said. He started moving his hips again and the movement this time was more purposeful. He wasn't teasing the both of them now. The beast within him had been woken and he held her hips with the strong grasp of his hand as he drew in and out of her body.

He did it slowly, letting her feel each inch as he pulled it out, then plunged back in until he was buried inside of her.

"Is that what you wanted?" he asked, his raspy voice sending chills down her spine.

"Yes, but more. Yesss…"

"Selena, you feel so good to me," he said, then lowered his head and kissed her deeply, his tongue thrusting into her mouth with the same rhythm of his hips. She held on to his shoulders to lift herself more fully into his embrace.

Every particle of her being was crying out for release but he was keeping her right on the edge. So that little climaxes feathered through her, making him thrust faster and harder. Plunging into her and driving her over the edge. She tore her mouth from his and screamed his name as her orgasm rushed through her.

Justin held her hips and drove into her three more times before shuddering in her arms and emptying himself in her body. She lifted herself against him once more to draw out the exquisite feeling of pleasure.

He leaned off her body to the side but still held her close and she liked it.

She turned her head to look up at him. "I…"

"Don't," he said. "Don't say anything."

"Is this a mistake?"

He rolled over and pulled her into his arms so she rested on his chest, right over his heart. It beat loudly under her ear. "You don't feel like a mistake to me. But I think objectivity is gone."

She knew he was right. "We can't pretend we are just vacation lovers."

"No, we can't. I've never been good at lying, even to myself and you feel like more than a temporary affair."

It felt the same to her. She wanted more.

Thirteen

A week later, Selena still hadn't made sense of anything with Justin. He was keeping his distance and on some levels, that worked for her. Her grandparents and the other vendors had all had their meetings with him at Luna Azul. Selena had participated in some of them but for the most part had stayed back.

She needed to read every contract that was offered and go over the details very carefully. She'd also spent a fair amount of time at the zoning office and realized that Justin already knew that as long as he hired a local contractor he was within his rights to start construction.

Selena advised everyone of this fact so that they realized at some point they needed to concede some of their dream-list demands.

Her cell phone rang just as she was driving away from her grandparents' store. She glanced at the caller ID and saw that it was Justin.

"Hello." She put him on her Bluetooth speakerphone.

"Put on your dancing shoes tonight, I'm taking you out."

"Really? Don't you think you should ask me first?"

"Nah, you'd just debate about it and then agree. I'm saving us a little time."

"Okay, then I guess I'll agree to go out with you. Where are we going?"

"Luna Azul. It's celebration time and you and I have never been to the club."

"Celebration?" she asked.

"Yes, ma'am. I finished the last of the appointments ten minutes ago and everyone is on board. Thank you for your hard work in making this happen."

"Not a problem. It is as important to you as it is to me."

"I know," he said. "That's why we need to celebrate. I will pick you up at seven and we can have dinner at my favorite restaurant first."

"Wait a minute. I can't do this," she said abruptly.

"Why not?"

She realized she was shaking and pulled the car over. "We were just a vacation fling, remember? We can't mix business and pleasure. We just can't."

"Why not?"

"Because if we do, I'm going to lose myself. I'm going to fall right back into the girl I used to be. I can't do that."

"You aren't going to turn into the girl you used to be. You're a woman now, Selena, successful and sure of yourself. There is no way you'd ever fall for a con again. And I'm not conning you. I've been nothing but honest with you."

That was true. "You have. But I haven't been honest with myself. I can't pretend that you mean nothing to me and I know we have no future. I can't stay here."

"Why not?"

"Because I have a life that I enjoy."

"Fair enough. Let's talk about this over dinner. I want to celebrate what we both worked so hard for. At least give me that," he said.

She realized that if she saw him again she was never going to be able to leave. He wouldn't let her and she was weak where he was concerned.

"Sounds good," she said, knowing that it was a lie. She wasn't going to meet Justin. In fact, if she played her cards right she'd never see him again. A clean break and she'd be back in New York in the heart of her safe life. Staying here…that wasn't an option no matter how tempting it might be.

She disconnected the call. She already knew about her grandparents' agreement with Luna Azul. There were only a few things left for her to do and then she could head home.

It was beyond time for her to leave. She was beginning to forget she had a life somewhere else. She'd fallen back into her old Miami routines but it wasn't the way she'd been before. She was eating breakfast with her grandparents, spending the afternoons with her brother and enjoying an idyllic life. But that wasn't realistic. If she moved back here, she'd be working all the time like she did back north. And why would she move here…for her family or for Justin?

She shook her head as she drove up to her hotel. It

had helped her keep her perspective that she was here temporarily, or had it? It was hard to stay because Justin had changed the way she looked at life here.

Granted, she was no longer the twenty-year-old woman who had left home with her tail between her legs. Helping her grandparents reclaim their grocery store and have a say in the new Mercado had helped resolve her leftover feelings of guilt.

She pulled the car over as the emotions she'd been burying for so long came to the surface. She started to cry.

She put her head down on the steering wheel. The flood of tears was gone and she felt vulnerable now. Justin had done this to her. He'd helped her make things right for her grandparents and for herself. She knew no one had blamed her for what Raul had done. But his actions had been a black specter over her for too many years and finally she was free.

She wiped her tears as she lifted her head. She had to get back to the hotel and get changed if she was going to actually go through with it and be on time to meet with Justin.

Justin.

He made her feel things she'd never experienced before. Not just sexually, she realized. Sex she could handle because that was lust and hormones—she could explain her attachment sexually to him. But the other bonds. The way she'd missed sleeping in his arms after only doing it one night—that wasn't right.

She was falling in love with him.

Love.

Oh, God, no. She wasn't ready to be in love with Justin Stern. She wasn't ready to face the future with him by her side…if he even wanted that. And what if he didn't?

She needed to get away. She drove to her hotel and handed her keys to the valet. Telling him to keep the car up front because she was checking out.

She went up to her room, packed her bags and called for a bellman. She wanted—no, needed—to get back to New York. Once she was away from Miami, the tropical fever that had been affecting her would go away. She'd be back to normal and whatever emotions she thought she was experiencing would go away.

It was just the vacation mind-set that was making her feel this way. She jotted a short note to Justin on the hotel stationery telling him she was needed at her job and left it at the front desk for him after she checked out.

Ten minutes later she was back in her car and headed to the airport. She knew that Justin would be upset that she left him that way but hey, he'd done it to her the other night, so…

She knew that leaving town wasn't the same as leaving her after a dinner. But at this moment it felt pretty darn close and though she knew her grandparents would be upset that she'd left again, she knew it was time to get out of here. And they at least would always love her.

Justin hung up the phone and leaned back in his leather executive chair. He glanced up at the portrait on the wall of him and his brothers with their father. It was the one thing he'd used as a talisman to keep himself focused on business.

But no matter how long he stared at it now, he knew that he'd been changed by this Mercado deal. He also realized that now that most of their business was concluded there was no real reason for Selena to stay in Miami, but he decided that he was going to ask her to stay. He had tried to keep things light but to be honest it wasn't his nature to be so casual. That was the main reason why he'd always limited himself to short-term affairs. But Selena wasn't that type of woman and with her at least he wasn't that kind of man.

He knew he wasn't ready for marriage...because he'd promised himself to never take that step. But he already knew that Selena meant more to him than any woman ever had.

She made him feel the same loyalty and devotion that he felt for his brothers but there was more than that where she was concerned. He didn't want to admit it to himself but he had fallen for her. He refused to say that it was love because he wouldn't be that weak. But it was pretty damned close.

Maybe knowing that was the key to not being like his father. The last thing he wanted was for Selena to realize how much she meant to him and how much control that gave her.

He got to his feet and walked to his office window. Miami was his hometown but he had seen a different side of it while he'd been with Selena. A side that made him realize that he'd been missing out on a few things.

Important things. He'd isolated himself here in the office. Tonight he was going to take the first step to break down the walls he'd used to shield himself all these years.

It was silly really but being a workaholic had meant that no one expected anything from him when it came to family. His brothers knew they'd have to call him at the office; his "friends" had all been colleagues. Until Selena. Now he was getting to know Enrique and Tomas and Paulo as friends.

He owed that all to Selena. Even though she thought she was no longer entrenched in her family, he'd seen that she was and she'd brought him into that group as well.

There was a knock on his door.

"Come in," he said.

Cam stood there looking tired but holding a bottle of Cristal in one hand and two champagne glasses in the other. "I figured it was time to celebrate."

"Definitely. I sent the last contract to legal and have a verbal confirmation from all of the vendors. To be honest, things worked out even better than I anticipated."

"I knew they would," Cam said. He put the glasses on the desk and opened the bottle of champagne.

"Is Nate coming?"

"No. He… I'm not sure what's going on with him. I think that he is doing something with Jen."

"Doesn't he always these days? He's taken to being a committed man like a fish to water."

"Yes, I hope he doesn't run into the Curse of the Stern men. We just aren't good with women and relationships," Cam said.

Justin took the champagne flute that Cam gave him. "To our success."

They both took a sip of the drink. Justin wished he could say that his mind was still on business but he knew that he was thinking of Selena and the Stern curse.

What if he was destined to screw up the relationship with her?

"Now about the tenth anniversary celebration..."

"Yes, we can get to work planning the details of the ground-breaking. Nate tells me most of the pieces are falling into place for the outdoor festival and concert."

"Excellent," Cam said. "That's exactly what I was hoping you'd say."

"I know. You are an even worse workaholic perfectionist than I am," Justin said.

"I'm not a workaholic," Cam said. "I just put the club and our company first."

Justin reached over and squeezed his brother's shoulder. "I know you do, but you're not on your own supporting us anymore. We are wealthy men, we're here to help. You could relax."

Cam nodded. "I don't know how to relax...or so I've been told."

"That's BS. I've heard the same thing said about myself. The problem with people who make those comments is that they don't understand what it's like to work hard to make their own business successful."

"I see your point, but I am almost always at work or at the club. I was thinking I might take a few days off."

Justin looked at his brother shrewdly. "Is there a woman involved?" Not because Justin was psychic or anything but Selena had made *him* behave that way.

"Maybe. Not sure. Why?"

"Don't you remember me moving into the Ritz?"

"Hell, yes. A woman?"

Justin nodded. "Selena Gonzalez."

"I like her," Cam said. "She's smart and funny. Is she staying in Miami?"

"I hope so. Now that our business is over I can concentrate on her...but I'm not sure that is the wisest thing to do."

"Why not?"

"The Stern curse. Look at Dad."

Cam shook his head. "You're not like Dad. Dad married our mother for business reasons. Even though they didn't get along, I think he liked not having a woman who'd take up his time."

"Why did he stay with her?"

Cam looked over at Justin. This was a subject they'd never spoken of before. "I think he stayed for us. I think having sons was something he hadn't expected."

"How do you know?"

"Just an educated guess. And I know you aren't like Dad when it comes to women," Cam said.

"I don't even know that."

"Jus, look at the life you have led," Cam said. "Then look at the fact that you went through a tough negotiation with Selena and kept your personal life separate. You got the job done. That takes a strong man. And I've always known you were that."

"Thanks, Cam. I...I'm scared to admit how much I need her."

"If she's half the woman I think she is, that won't be a problem. It wasn't Dad's devotion that was the issue with our parents but rather Mother's coldness. Selena isn't like that, is she?"

Justin thought about that after his brother left. If there was one thing he knew for sure it was that Selena wasn't cold. And he wasn't a man who gave up when he wanted something as badly as he wanted her.

* * *

As much as Selena wanted to just escape to the airport and head back to New York, she knew she had to at least read over the contracts with all the vendors for the Mercado one last time. So she was sitting in the back room of her grandfather's grocery store, poring over the documents.

She'd gotten lucky that her grandfather was busy with customers and hadn't had a chance to notice her suitcases in the rental car. She knew she'd have to tell him that she was leaving, but right now she just needed to focus on business. So she read the contracts and existed in a world where emotions weren't a part of the equation. The Stern brothers had been more than fair in the agreements, but she refused to let herself dwell on that or on Justin.

She had had to pay an insane amount of money for the ticket and even then her flight didn't leave for another six hours. Once she was on the plane and back in her Upper West Side apartment, she'd relax. Until then she was swamped with an overwhelming sense of panic. She was afraid. Not of her family or Justin or even how they'd react when they realized she'd left, but of herself.

She didn't want to go. Last time she'd left she wanted to leave. Couldn't have gotten out of Miami fast enough. But this time she wanted to stay and that was even more dangerous.

She knew that the life she'd been living here wasn't real and that getting back to her routine was the only thing that would wake her up. Smiling and laughing and doing things that made no sense like sleeping with Justin Stern…that wasn't her and she needed to get back to New York where she could remember who she was.

"Selena?"

She started as she heard her name and turned to see Paulo standing there. She got up and gave her cousin a hug.

"I think I already reviewed your contract," she said.

"You did," he said. "I noticed your suitcase in the car. Are you leaving?"

"Yes, I am. I was just here to make sure that Luna Azul didn't take advantage of you all in the fine print. I'm almost done."

"I must have missed *abuelita*'s call. I thought she was going to have everyone over before you went back home."

Selena flushed as a weird sensation made her stomach feel like it was full of lead. "Uh, I kind of haven't told her I'm leaving yet."

"What? What's going on? Are you okay?" he asked.

"Nothing is going on. I just got word that all of the vendors at the Mercado were ready to sign their contracts and there is no reason for me to stay anymore."

"No reason...what about family?" Paulo asked.

"I am not leaving the family, Paulo. I'm—"

"Is this about that guy you were dating?" he asked.

"No. The guy—Justin—he's not responsible for this," she said. She needed to make sure her family understood that what was going on had nothing to do with Justin and everything to do with her. "I have to get back to my job, that's all."

"Your job?" Paulo asked. "Maybe if I hadn't known you since we were in diapers I'd believe that. But to leave without saying anything to our grandparents... *Tata,* that is not like you. Even after Raul you said goodbye to them."

She shook her head. "If I don't leave now, Paulo, I think I'm going to make an even bigger mistake than I did before."

He hugged her close to him. "What kind of mistake? I can help you."

She pulled back and realized how much she really loved her family. "You can't. I wish you could."

"There is nothing that is so big that you have to run away."

"I know it seems like I'm running away, but truly I'm not, Paulo, I'm simply going home."

"Is New York really your home?" he asked.

"Yes," she said with all the confidence she could muster. She wanted Paulo to believe it because maybe if he did, she would.

"That's a lie, *tata*," he said. "When you came down here you were buttoned up, wearing all black and looking like anyone else from up there. But after a few days your hair was down and you blossomed back into the woman you really are."

"I haven't changed," she said.

"Then you aren't being honest with yourself. I hope you wake up to the fact that you can't ever really be comfortable in your own skin unless you acknowledge that your family is a huge part of who you are," he said.

Paulo was being hard on her. Almost as hard as she was sure her grandparents would be. "I'm not going to change my mind."

"I hope someday you do. When are you calling *abuelita?*"

"I will do it in a few minutes when I've finished reviewing this last contract."

"Make sure you do. I don't want to keep secrets for you."

Paulo walked away and she shivered. If she wasn't so afraid she'd try to find a way to stay, but there were no doubts in her mind that she needed to go back home and get some perspective. But Paulo had a point and for the first time she'd seen how badly it had hurt her family the way she'd left before, but they had understood. If Paulo was that mad, how would Enrique and her grandparents react?

How would Justin?

What was she running from? Was she making a huge mistake?

She rubbed the back of her neck. She shouldn't leave without at least saying goodbye to her grandparents. She couldn't. "Paulo!"

"Si, tata?"

"Will you come with me to *abuelita's*?"

"Definitely. I think this is the right thing to do."

"Paulo, I'm so confused. No one has ever made me feel this way."

"You mean Justin?"

"Yes. And he's not…he's not like anyone else I've ever known. I'm afraid to trust myself."

"You shouldn't be. You are a very smart woman, *tata*," Paulo said. A few minutes later they were in his car driving toward her grandparents' house.

Selena wanted to pretend that she was still getting on that airplane and leaving Miami but a part of her no longer wanted to go.

* * *

Justin arrived at the Ritz twenty minutes before he was supposed to pick Selena up. He went to his room and packed up his luggage and had it taken to his car before he went to check out. Selena was going to look right at home in his waterfront house on Fisher Island. It would be nice to see her there.

"How can I help you, sir?"

"I'm checking out," he said. "Justin Stern."

The front desk hostess nodded and started working on her computer and a minute later glanced up and smiled at him. "It says we have a letter for you. Let me grab that while you look over the folio."

She handed him his resort bill and he glanced down at it before signing his name. Then she passed him an envelope and told him to have a nice day.

The handwriting on the front was Selena's and he knew what it said before he even opened it.

But he tore it open anyway. He glanced down at the note on the hotel stationery.

Justin,
I have an emergency back in New York and had to catch a flight out today. Thank you for all of your hard work on making the Luna Azul Mercado a true part of the Cuban American community. I wish you much success with this endeavor.
　　On a personal note, I'm sorry to leave without seeing you again but I think this might be easier. I have come to care for you and am questioning my own judgment where you are concerned. Forgive me. I know deep down you'll understand.

Please accept my apology for not calling you but I was afraid to hear your voice again before I left.

Take care,
Selena

Justin refolded the letter and put it in his pocket as he walked out of the club. He got in his Porsche 911 and drove like a madman away from the Ritz. He had no real destination in mind until he found himself parked in front of Selena's house.

He remembered the night they'd made love by her pool. The night that had changed everything between them and though he'd thought he had the luxury of time to make up his mind about her and what he wanted from their relationship, he just realized that Selena was battling the same things he had been. And she'd decided that a quick, clean break was the simplest solution.

But he knew it wasn't. She thought that now that she'd gotten everything she wanted that she could walk away from him, and he felt used.

He'd been the one who'd started this and he'd be the one to end it. Justin Stern wasn't her lapdog…he wasn't about to let Selena get what she wanted and then walk away.

He fired up the engine of his car and drove back to his office building. If that was the way she wanted to play things then he would show her that he was more than willing to play her game. And he would beat her at it.

He pulled out the contracts and then had his assistant bring him the list of other local business owners who weren't in the Mercado. The zoning ordinance simply said that it had to be a local vendor, not that it had to be the same ones.

He drew up a list of comparable businesses and then called Cam to tell him to hold off on celebrating.

"Why?" Cam asked.

"Because we're not going to be lying down for the committee. If they want to be a part of the Mercado they will have to meet our terms," Justin said.

"What has changed in the last two hours? And how much is it going to cost us to break the contracts with our current vendors?"

Justin knew he had to tell his brother something but he didn't have the words right now. "I will tell you later. Let's just say that I think an expert played us. And that makes me mad."

"What does Selena say?"

"I have no idea, she's gone back to New York."

There was silence on the line and Justin knew he'd said too much.

"You can't go back on the deals we have in place. I know you are angry. Hell, I'm pissed for you, but there is no way we are going to let a woman ruin the good thing we have going."

"I know. I really know that it's not the best idea, but I want to hurt her, Cam."

"I understand that," Cam said. "I'm coming back to the office. Don't do anything rash."

When Cam ended the call, Justin stood up, trying to get rid of the restless energy that was making him feel like he was going to punch something. He wasn't in the right frame of mind to work right now, he knew that, but he had no idea where he would go.

The gym. He needed physical exercise and a lot of

it. He would love it if he could go to a boxing ring but the closet one was thirty minutes away and he wasn't in any shape to drive right now.

He kept a bag of workout clothes at the office and grabbed them and his iPod and left. The gym was only a block away and he walked there, got changed and was on the treadmill in less than twenty minutes.

He put his headphones on and ran. It took about two miles for his mind to settle down and he realized that revenge was not the smartest reaction to have to her leaving.

He cared too much for Selena. He knew that he wanted to hurt her the way she'd hurt him by leaving with only a note to explain her actions. But he also liked Tomas and Paulo and all of the other business owners. Hurting them might succeed in getting Selena's attention but he wasn't interested in ruining Luna Azul and his new friends in the process.

"Want some company?" Cam asked as he walked up. He got on the treadmill next to Justin and started running.

"No, but I don't think you are going to listen to me."

"I'm not," Cam said.

"How did you find me here?"

"You're pretty predictable, bro." Cam took a long look at Justin before he started up the machine. "Are you still thinking like a knucklehead?"

"No. I know I can't throw away everything we've worked for because of a woman."

"Good. What else have you figured out?"

"I still want her, Cam. Maybe this is what Dad felt

about Mother. Maybe he realized that he couldn't live without her."

"Maybe, little brother, I never understood the two of them. But this is about you."

How true. He didn't care about his parents' relationship; it was time to break the cycle. He realized he wasn't interested in doing anything that was going to harm Selena. He wanted her back. When he had her in his arms again, he'd make damned sure she never left.

Selena was his. She'd made that choice when she'd given herself to him on his yacht. He hadn't realized it at the time but a bond had been formed.

It took him two more miles of running on the treadmill until he had the seeds of a plan. Normally he'd play his cards close to his chest and keep this wound private but he knew to win Selena he was going to have to pull out all of the stops and involve not only his family but hers as well.

As Justin stepped off the treadmill, he turned to Cam with a smile on his face.

Fourteen

Selena was cold. It was almost April and though spring had definitely been present in Miami, it wasn't very warm here in Manhattan. She'd been back for one weekend. That was it, even though it felt like a lifetime.

She pulled her coat a little closer as she exited the subway station nearest her office and started walking. There were a lot of people on the street but she kept her head down and just walked.

Selena's talk with her grandparents and brother the day she left had been…somber, but she'd done what needed doing. Her boss had been very happy to see her back from her leave of absence so soon and had immediately put her on a project.

The kind of project she loved, one where she just worked 24/7 and was consumed with all the research she had to do. Being a corporate lawyer meant lots of time reading case studies and finding precedence.

She wanted to believe she'd made the right choice but she felt alone and missed Justin. He hadn't called her and to be honest she hadn't expected him to. She hadn't really given him an opening to.

She entered her office and walked past the security guard flashing her badge. He smiled at her as he did every day and called good morning to her. But she didn't smile back. She just didn't have it in her to pretend to be happy when she wasn't.

She took the elevator to the seventh floor where her office was and when she was seated behind her desk she looked around.

She shook her head as she waited for her computer to boot up.

What was she doing here?

Waiting.

She'd spent her entire life waiting.

Her phone rang and she glanced at the caller ID. It was her brother.

She picked up and said, "Hi, Enrique."

"I'm sorry to bother you at work but we need you back in Florida."

"Why? What is going on?"

"The Stern brothers have offered me a gig. I want you to be here. It's my first legit gig," Enrique said.

"When is it?"

"This weekend. I know you said you needed to be back in New York, but I really want you here for this."

"Let me see what I can do," she said. She couldn't avoid the important events in her brother's life. "I will let you know if I'm coming."

"*Tata,* I need my sister there. We are all each other has."

"Enrique, you have *abuelito* and *abuelita* there."

"It's not the same. I want my big sister to be here."

"Okay, I'll do it."

"Good."

They hung up and she stared at the phone. It was odd that her grandfather hadn't told her about the gig when they spoke on the phone last night. But he was still mad she'd left and had refused to tell her anything about the Mercado, so that might explain it.

She went online to research airfares and almost booked her flight, but she realized if she was going back she wanted to see Justin. She needed to see him. She picked up the phone and dialed Justin's number. Something she'd done numerous times in the past. But this time she hung up before he answered. The same thing stopped her now, as had each time over the last several days.

What was she going to say to him? She honestly had no idea what he was going to be like when she phoned. If she knew she'd get his voice mail she'd stay on the line even if just to listen to his voice. And if he answered she could make up some excuse about wanting to read Enrique's contract for him or find out how the Mercado was progressing but that wasn't the truth.

She missed him.

There, she'd said it.

Since she'd been back, she'd been existing.

Existing…hadn't she always wanted more from her life?

Her boss walked by and paused in the doorway.

"You look like you are pondering something big."

"I am. I think I am going to resign."

"Why?"

"I don't belong here, Rudy, I need to be back in Miami."

He shook his head. "I knew I shouldn't have let my best lawyer go to Miami in March."

"It's not the weather," she said.

"What is it then?"

No way was she going to tell her boss that it was a man. A man who might not even want her after the way she'd left. She'd made a mistake but if Justin had cared for her even a tenth as much as she loved him, then he would at least listen to her and that was all she needed.

Her time in Miami had reawakened her fighting spirit.

"It's my heart. I left it down there and I don't think I'm surviving very well without it."

He nodded. "That I understand. Can you at least finish the case you are working on?"

If she worked around the clock she could get her research finished and her notes in order so that she could pass it on to another attorney. She nodded and got to work.

Suddenly she didn't feel so lethargic. She looked out the window, realizing soon she'd be back home in Miami and that was really all she needed.

She decided she'd go to Miami for Enrique's gig this coming weekend. It would give her a chance to find Justin and try to make amends before she moved back there permanently. And if she hustled, she could finish her move by the time Luna Azul's tenth anniversary party rolled around.

She didn't want to waste any more time now that she'd decided what she wanted. She felt silly that it had taken her so long to realize that Justin owned her heart. She suspected she'd known it when she'd gotten on that plane in Miami to fly back here.

When Justin got off the private plane Hutch Damien had loaned him and walked across the tarmac to the heliport, he thanked his lucky stars. Nate's celebrity friends sure came in handy.

Flying to New York City had been his last resort. At first he'd harbored a few fantasies of Selena coming crawling back to him but those had died quickly.

Given her past with men, he knew he was going to have to compromise and be the one to make the first move. He was still mad at the way she'd run off. But he loved her. He'd known that almost the instant he'd read her letter and realized that she was leaving him.

It had taken him one lonely night before he was able to admit it out loud and then he knew that he had to get her back. On his own. He knew her family was more than willing to help him get her to come back, but this was strictly between him and her.

There was no way he could spend the rest of his life without her.

His cell phone rang before he got on the chopper for his ride to midtown Manhattan and Selena's office.

"Stern."

"It's Tomas. Enrique called Selena this morning and… told her about the gig. I think she is coming home."

"Dammit. I told Enrique I could do this without his help," Justin said.

"He loves his sister and he wants her to be happy."

Of that Justin had no doubt. "I thought I said I was handling this."

"You did but our family doesn't want to leave anything to chance."

Justin shook his head. "Thanks for letting me know. I will call as soon as I have some news."

"Just bring our *tata* home," Tomas said.

Justin had every intention of doing just that. Selena belonged by his side. Together they had made a good team but they had also completed each other. This wasn't some big show to convince her to overlook his flaws. She hadn't changed who he was at his core; she'd just shown him that the right woman was all he needed to be happy.

Years of short-term affairs had left him with the feeling that he was just like his father. But one month with the right woman had convinced him that he had been wrong.

He needed Selena the way he needed to breathe.

He got on the chopper and watched the views as he flew over Manhattan. Not bad. What he hadn't told her family but had told his brothers was that if Selena wouldn't come back to Miami, he was going to move here. He even had a possible apartment lined up just in case.

The chopper landed at the heliport and his driver met Justin. Soon they were on their way to Selena's office.

He knew her well enough to know that she would be at work even though it was almost six in the evening. She was the kind of person who poured herself into whatever task she took. But more than that, she'd run away not only from him but also from her family. It was going to take a lot of work to keep her mind busy so she wouldn't have to think of all she'd left behind.

Tonight she was going to have no choice but to think about it. He was back. And he was going to get the answers he needed from her about her actions and then he was going to find the key to both of their happiness.

He was sure it was in the both of them. That they belonged together. Now all he had to do was convince her of that.

His phone buzzed and he glanced down to see a text message from his brother.

Cam: Are you there?
Justin: Just.
Cam: Let me know how it goes.

Justin had to laugh. One would think a make-or-break business deal hung in the balance the way Tomas and Cam were anxiously awaiting news. But he knew that both men had his best personal interest at heart. This wasn't about business.

Justin: I will.

Cam had been worried, angry and then understanding when Justin had come to him and told him that he had to go to Manhattan and that there was a chance he was going to move there.

It had taken Cam less than twenty-four hours to figure out a plan to keep Justin in the business no matter where he ended up. He wanted to bring what he called "a taste of Miami Latin to the club scene in Manhattan" and Justin would be in charge of finding a new location and getting it up and running if he decided to stay in New York.

When the driver pulled to a stop in front of Selena's

building, Justin jumped out of the car. He entered the skyscraper and went right up to the security guard at the reception desk.

"Can I help you, sir?"

"I'd like to see Selena Gonzalez," he said, and gave the man the name of her law firm.

"Is she expecting you?" the guard asked.

"No, she isn't." Never in a million years. But then he figured she didn't know him as well as she should have. How much he needed her. If she had, she might not have ever left him in Miami.

"Have a seat over there, sir."

Justin walked a few feet from the desk but couldn't sit down. Not now. He was ready to see Selena and no matter what happened he wasn't leaving this building until he did.

The guard hung up the phone and motioned for him to come over. Justin did and was handed a pass and given instructions on how to get to Selena's office.

Selena hung up the phone and immediately pulled out her compact and checked her makeup. It was shallow, she knew, but she wanted to be looking her best when Justin got up here. She reapplied her lipstick but there was no disguising the dark circles under her eyes. She was tired and he was going to be able to tell without much effort.

She could hardly believe he was here. What if she'd imagined the call? All day she'd thought about the fact that if she moved back to Miami there was a very real chance for her to reconcile with him.

Reconcile? She would probably have to get down on her knees and beg him to give her another chance. And she was in a place in her life right now to do that. She wanted Justin. He was the reason she was quitting her job and moving back to Miami.

She heard the outer door of her office open and got to her feet, poking her head around the corner.

Justin.

He looked better than she'd remembered. His hair was casually tousled, his skin tanner than the last time she'd seen him and his eyes very intense.

She had to force herself to stay in the doorway and not run to him. But she wanted a hug. She needed one. She hadn't had a single good night's sleep since she left him and she craved the feeling of those big strong arms around her.

"Hello," she said.

"Thanks for agreeing to see me," he said.

She stepped back and retreated behind her desk as he walked toward her. But when he entered the room she realized she wasn't in a position of power, not anymore. She'd tried to protect herself by leaving Miami but she was completely vulnerable where Justin was concerned.

She'd give him whatever he wanted if he forgave her.

"I figured it was the least I could do."

He tipped his head to the side. "The very least…why did you run away?"

"I was scared. I guess I didn't want to take a chance on staying and letting you hurt me."

"Why would I have hurt you?"

"Because all the men in my life have. Maybe not my *abuelito*. But my papa died when I needed him the most and Raul took my heart and my money and then he left. I didn't want to give you the chance to do the same thing to me. So when I realized our business was done and that I had a small window of time to get out of Miami—I took it."

"Have I ever done anything to make you think I would leave you like that?" he asked.

"You suggested we have a vacation affair. That we pretend that our lives were separate. That isn't exactly a ringing endorsement for giving your heart to someone."

"You were afraid of me and what I made you feel. From the beginning it was me coming on strong and you backing up. I guess I should have expected you to run."

Selena looked at him and saw the man she loved. Saw the pain she'd caused him when she'd left. If she had to guess, she'd say it wasn't just the leaving but the way she'd done it. Sneaking out of Miami the way Raul had done to her.

"I'm sorry."

"Me, too."

"Why are you sorry?"

"That you felt you had to leave like that."

"I care for you—hell, I love you, Justin, but I'm not sure I can trust any man with my heart. I ran away from everyone because the desire to stay was so strong I couldn't trust it."

"You love me?" he asked her.

She nodded. There was no way she was going to deny it. She wanted Justin back in her life and he realized it would take a lot for him to trust her again but it was what she wanted more than anything else.

"Yes, I do."

"I'm still angry at you for running away," he said.

"I expected as much. I don't know if I'd be able to forgive myself."

"I can forgive you, I understood why you left even as you were running away. But the anger is still there."

She nodded. "I understand. By the way, why are you here? Enrique said you gave him a gig. I was going to call you and tell you I'm coming back to Miami."

"That is good to hear. Enrique is trying to be helpful. I guess I didn't move fast enough for your family. They want you back."

"Of course they do," she said, relieved that Justin was the kind of man she'd believed him to be. Not a man who would try to hurt her family because she hurt him. "But do you?"

"I wouldn't be here if I didn't."

She smiled over at him. "Thank God. I know it's going to take time before you and I can be back to the way we were…I've already talked to my boss about resigning and moving home. I think—"

"No. You don't have to resign and move back to Miami. I am here because I can't stand another day without you. Together we will figure out what works for both of us because I'm not letting you leave me again."

"Why?"

"Because I love you."

She jumped up and ran around her desk and threw herself into his arms, kissing him. He squeezed her tightly to him and she almost started crying. She'd thought she could control her emotions but she couldn't.

"I was afraid to dream this could happen. I really didn't know what to expect."

"I knew what was going to happen. I have fallen in love with one woman in my life and that's you. There was no way I was going to let you go. I need you, Selena. You are the one person who grounds me."

She cupped his face with her hands and kissed him again. "I need you, too, Justin. You make it possible for me to believe in my dreams again."

"Good. Now what do you say we get out of here so I can make love to you."

"Sounds like a very good idea," she said.

Justin took her hand in his but stopped. "I am not leaving here until you answer one more question."

She took a deep breath. "Yes."

"Will you marry me?"

Justin wasn't playing around. He wasn't about to get Selena back in his life only to let her walk away again. He needed her to not only be his but to show the world that she was.

"Are you sure?"

"I wouldn't have asked if I wasn't," he said. He reached into his pocket and pulled out the ring box. He opened it and took the ring out. "I know that proper form means I should be down on one knee, but I wanted to look into your eyes when you answer me." He'd had it specially made for her. A marquis-cut diamond that he knew would look perfect on her hand.

She nodded. "Yes, I will marry you."

He slipped the ring onto her finger and then pulled her close for a kiss. She moved against him.

And he leaned back against the door pulling her closer to him. He wanted this woman. She'd turned his world upside down and now that he had her back in his arms, he needed to reinforce those bonds by making her his.

"Are you really mine?" he asked.

She smiled up at him, grinning ear-to-ear. "I am."

She shifted against him and he hardened instantly. "Then let's get out of here and find a proper bed so I can make love to you."

She flushed and raised an eyebrow at him. "You drive a hard bargain. Give me a minute to get my bag and shut down my computer and we'll go to my place."

"Okay," he said. "Are you ready to go yet?"

"I am."

The ride across town to her apartment took too long and he held her on his lap and kissed her the entire time. He didn't want to stop touching her and luckily didn't have to.

She shifted around so that she was facing him instead of lying in his arms. "Thank you for coming after me. I mean, I was going to come to you, but thanks."

"You're welcome. I was angry at first and wanted revenge. But that just made me realize how much I love you—because I could never do anything to hurt you or your family."

She hugged him close. "I know you couldn't. Even though you are tough in business, you have a good heart."

"Selena, I thought I was the Tin Man until you came along and showed me that I had one."

The car came to a stop. "This is my place."

"About damned time," he said.

The doorman came and opened the door for them. Justin followed Selena into the lobby and onto the elevator. He couldn't resist caressing the curve of her hips and pulling her into his arms for another kiss. Then he lifted her in his arms as the elevator doors opened and carried her down the hallway, following her directions.

As soon as she unlocked her apartment door and then stepped inside he leaned back against it and kissed her with all the carnality he'd been bottling up since she'd agreed to be his wife.

She dropped her bag and kicked off her shoes as he walked into the apartment.

"Bedroom?"

"Down the hall. Take your jacket off," she said.

"I'd have to put you down and I'm not ready to do that yet."

He walked into her bedroom and set her in the center of her king-size bed. It was covered with pillows. When she turned on the bedside lamp he saw that her room was done in warm hues of green and gold.

He toed off his shoes and socks and then took off his jacket. She reached for the buttons at the front of her blouse but he brushed her fingers aside and undid them himself.

He took his time stripping her. Each new bit of skin that was revealed he took the time to caress first with his hands, then with his mouth.

He lingered over her breasts and when she got restless and tried to hurry him, he refused. This time he wanted it to last and knowing that he had the right to make love to her for the rest of his life gave him the willpower to take his time.

"Now you are mine," he said.

She unbuttoned his shirt and pushed it off his shoulders onto the floor. Her hands roamed over his chest and traced the path of hair down to his belly button. She ran the edge of her nail around the circumference of it again and again. Each circle she completed made him harden even more. She reached for his pants and quickly had them open.

"Now *you're* mine, Justin."

Luckily, they would have a lifetime to work through the fine points of this negotiation.

Epilogue

At the end of May, after Selena had tied up all the loose ends in New York, she and Justin flew down to Miami for the ground-breaking of the Mercado and Luna Azul's tenth anniversary party. The guest list consisted of a glittering array of celebrities. But Selena didn't really care about that. This afternoon, she was enjoying herself in the warm Miami sunshine. They were having a party at her grandparents' house to celebrate her engagement to Justin.

"How's my fiancée?" he asked, coming up behind her and wrapping his arm around her waist.

"Good. I never thought I'd feel this at home in Miami, but moving back here with you…it feels right."

"We can always go back to New York. I'm up to the challenge of opening a Luna Azul club there."

"No, Justin. I'm here to stay." Selena was quiet for

a moment. Then, looking deep into his eyes, she said, "Thank you."

"For what?"

"For giving me back what I thought I'd lost forever."

"What was that?"

"My family and my heritage," she said.

"I didn't give it back to you, you helped me find it and now we can share that. I think we both ended up winning."

"I think so, too," Selena said, going up on her tiptoes and kissing Justin.

"I told you he was a good man," her *abuelita* said as she came up behind her.

"That's not all you said," Selena said with a grin.

"What else did she say?" Tomas asked.

"That he had a nice butt, *abuelito!*"

Justin flushed and everyone standing around them started laughing.

"Well, he does," her grandmother said.

"I guess you are part of the family now," Cam said to Justin. "They definitely like you."

"I like them, too," Justin admitted. He pulled Selena close and whispered in her ear. "I love you."

"I love you, too, Justin Stern."

* * * * *

Silhouette Desire

COMING NEXT MONTH

Available April 12, 2011

#2077 A WIFE FOR A WESTMORELAND
Brenda Jackson
The Westmorelands

#2078 BOUGHT: HIS TEMPORARY FIANCÉE
Yvonne Lindsay
The Takeover

#2079 REUNITED...WITH CHILD
Katherine Garbera
Miami Nights

#2080 THE SARANTOS SECRET BABY
Olivia Gates
Billionaires and Babies

#2081 HER INNOCENCE, HIS CONQUEST
Jules Bennett

#2082 THE PRINCE'S PREGNANT BRIDE
Jennifer Lewis
Royal Rebels

REQUEST YOUR FREE BOOKS!

2 FREE NOVELS
PLUS 2
FREE GIFTS!

Silhouette®

Desire®

Passionate, Powerful, Provocative!

*Selene wanted nothing to do with the father of her son,
Alex; but Aristedes had other plans...that included them.*

*Read on for an sneak peek from
THE SARANTOS SECRET BABY by Olivia Gates,
available April 2011, only from Harlequin Desire.*

"You were right to turn my marriage offer down," Aristedes said.

And Selene found her voice at last, found the words that
would not betray the blow he'd dealt her. "Thanks for letting me know. You didn't have to come all the way here,
though. You could have just let it go. I left yesterday with
the understanding that this case is closed."

Before the hot needles behind her eyes could dissolve
into an unforgivable display of stupidity and weakness, she
began to close the door.

The door stopped against an immovable object. His flat palm.

"I can't accept that." His voice was low, leashed.

What did her tormentor mean now? Was he ending one
game only to start another?

She raised eyes as bruised as her self-respect to his,
found nothing there but solemnity and determination.

Before she could voice her confusion, he elaborated. "I
never let anything go unless I'm certain it's unworkable. I
realize I made you an unworkable offer, and that's why I'm
withdrawing it. I'm here to offer something else. A work-
ability study."

She leaned against the door, thankful for its support and
partial shield. "Your son and I are not a business venture
you can test for feasibility."

His gaze grew deeper, made her feel as if he was trying
to delve into her mind, take control of it. "It's actually the

other way around. I'm the one who would be tested."

She shook her head. "Why bother? I know—and *you* know—you're not workable. Not with me."

His spectacular eyebrows lowered over eyes she felt were emitting silver hypnosis. "You're right again. Neither you nor I have any reason to believe that isn't the truth. The only truth. It might be best for both you and Alex to never hear from me again, to forget I exist. But then again, maybe not. I'm only asking for the chance for both of us to find out for certain. You believe I'm unworkable in any personal relationship. I've lived my life based on that belief about myself. I never really had reason to question it. But I have one now. In fact, I have two."

Find out what happens in
THE SARANTOS SECRET BABY by Olivia Gates,
available April 2011, only from Harlequin Desire.

Harlequin *Blaze*

red-hot reads

Sunny, sensual Hawaiian spring break…again!

Three best girlfriends are recapturing an amazing spring-break
vacation they had a decade ago.

First on the beach is former attorney and all-around good girl
Mia Butterfield. Meeting up with her boyfriend of old is a bust,
so she's shocked when her hero turns out to be someone she'd
never have expected…

Find out who it is in
SECOND TIME LUCKY
by acclaimed author
Debbi Rawlins

Available from Harlequin Blaze® April 2011

Part of the sensual miniseries,
Spring Break

Part 2: Delicious Do-Over (May)

Harlequin

A *Romance* FOR EVERY MOOD™

www.eHarlequin.com

HB79607